E V A
THE FUGITIVE

LATIN AMERICAN LITERATURE AND CULTURE

General Editor
Roberto González Echevarría
R. Selden Rose Professor of Spanish and
Professor of Comparative Literature
Yale University

E V A
THE FUGITIVE

(Eva y La Fuga)

ROSAMEL DEL VALLE

translated, with an introduction by
ANNA BALAKIAN

UNIVERSITY OF CALIFORNIA PRESS
Berkeley Los Angeles Oxford

University of California Press
Berkeley and Los Angeles, California

University of California Press
Oxford, England

Library of Congress Cataloging-in-Publication Data

Valle, Rosamel del, 1900–1965
    [Eva y la fuga. English]
    Eva, the fugitive / by Rosamel del Valle ; translated, with an introduction by Anna Balakian.
        p.   cm.—(Latin American literature and culture ; 5)
    ISBN 0-520-06850-5 (alk. paper).
    — ISBN 0-520-07116-6 (pbk. : alk. paper)
    I. Title. II. Series: Latin American literature and culture (Berkeley, Calif.) ; 5.
    PQ8098.32.A54E913   1990
    863—dc20   90-10752
                                        CIP

Printed in the United States of America

1 2 3 4 5 6 7 8 9

The paper used in this publication meets the minimum requirements of American National Standard for Information Sciences—Permanence of Paper for Printed Library Materials, ANSI Z39.48-1984 ∞

CONTENTS

INTRODUCTION

Born in 1901 in Curacavi, Chile, of half Spanish and half American Indian ancestry, Rosamel del Valle led a double-barreled life. The first part he spent among the young literati of Santiago in the years when surrealism was emerging in Europe. Having lost his father at age seventeen, he was totally self-directed in his acquisition of a tremendous reading repertoire that included European philosophers and poets of the nineteenth century, a thorough grounding in classical literature, and a comprehensive knowledge of the literature of the United States. He kept current on a daily basis with the then emerging literatures of the avant-garde both at home and abroad. He was a close friend of his poet-compatriots Vicente Huidobro, Pablo Neruda, and Humberto Díaz Casanueva (who, after Rosamel's death, during the Allende regime was to become his country's ambassador to the United Nations). At the same time, Rosamel lived so vicariously and thoroughly in the distant climate of Paris surrealists that he included their reading lists in his own, even to the extent of reading some of their idiosyncratic favorites, such as Edward Young's *Nights*, which I suspect he read in the French translation as did Paul Éluard and André Breton. He kept track of every new publication of the surrealists and translated a number of them into Spanish, including what is perhaps Breton's linguistically most difficult text, *Fata Morgana*.

Rosamel del Valle's first jobs had been at the printing press of *La Ilustración* and as a reporter for the daily *La Nación*. Although living on menial jobs, he managed to launch his own short-lived journals, such as *Ariel* in 1925 and *Panorama* in 1926. He assumed the role of social and literary journalist and in 1945 worked for the Postal and Telegraph Services; all the while he enjoyed the magic of daily effervescences in café gatherings with the stimulation of friends and of liquor.

He was not only self-taught but also self-named. His real name was Moisés Gutiérrez. He created the pen name of Rosamel del Valle by appropriating the name of an early sweetheart who was called Rosa Amelia del Valle, an early indication of the two parallel lives he was to live. As Señor Gutiérrez he spent some of his life in New York, as a member of the Secretariat of the United Nations, at the United Nations Department of Publications, and as the husband of Thérèse Dulac, the beautiful Canadian-French coworker whom he married in 1948.

In those years in New York, as the poet Rosamel he enjoyed being in the big city. Unlike the standard exile or diplomatic corps personnel, he felt part of his foreign environment, mingling with the cosmopolitan group at the UN but also seeking to know every corner of mystery in the five boroughs which might evoke the great American writers such as Whitman, Poe, Henry James, Willa Cather, Washington Irving, and Eugene O'Neill, all of whom he apparently had read very closely, and for whom he expressed great admiration. He traced their paths through landmarks such as those in Greenwich Village and wrote about them in various Spanish-language periodicals, principally in *La Nación*, *La Hora*, and *La Cronica*. He exercised three métiers simultaneously: besides his nine-to-five job at the UN publications office, he served as a reporter for Hispano-American newspapers and journals, and rising every morning at five he wrote steadily—poetry, essays, stories—utilizing that talent that made the rest of his waking hours glow in a magic *clima*.

New York suited his personality perfectly; it was for

him a place where one could be a totally private person and at the same time communicate with people and with things. Ordinary beings and urban sites and events would assume an aura for him, draw him as if magnetized, create labyrinthine secrets; in fact, New York functioned for him as Paris did for the European surrealists. Peril was metaphysical and not associated with squalor in the urban sites. Being at times solitary had nothing to do with being lonely, and there was no inconsistency between loving Santiago, his native city, and being enchanted by New York—a place for infinite exploration. I do not know of an American writer (of the USA) who has endowed New York with such magic as did Rosamel del Valle in the poetry and prose he wrote there. He was so happy in his cozy apartment at 209 East Sixty-Sixth Street that he was very disappointed to have to take mandatory retirement from the UN at age sixty. In 1962 he and his wife returned to Santiago, where they bought a house, but his retirement in the company of his old friends was of short duration. Having suffered the deaths of his mother and several of his friends in rapid succession, he died in his sleep— Thérèse would say "in his dreams"—in 1965, at age sixty-four.

So much to give a sense of the biographical contours of a life that was much more complicated in what he calls *hecho*, for want of a better word—that is, things, events, happenings in the interior sphere of his *consciencia* (awareness, consciousness, sense of being) than in anything that befell him from the outside.

I have a feeling as I read his essays as well as the work here translated that he was always closer to surrealism than to magic realism. In one of his essays he finds the term "magic realism" redundant, for, as he says, all reality is magic if the spirit that confronts such reality consists of a sense of mystery and a tongue of fire. What he supports in the surrealists is their affinity with the deranged, their scrutiny of ordinary detail in the concrete world around them, the cryptic use of language that allows for transformational possibilities—or, as he says in one of his essays, the possibility of accepting the possibility and the impossibility of each phenomenon. He invents his own special definitions of common words like *tornasol*, which is a sunflower but also resembles a rainbow—but the phenomenon *tornasol* is more than either a sunflower or a rainbow; it is a form of metamorphosis whereby the power of magic transforms existence. Then there is *pozo*, a well that in his case is both full and empty, a source of creativity and of subterfuge, bearing all the contradictions of the human personality; there is also a bird that talks, and companions who, one is not sure, may or may not really exist—because they fade out like dreams—and *asfixia*, which characterizes a general sense of malaise combined with the exhilaration that he feels at the immanent impact of an encounter with certain persons, objects, and places, and particularly with the semi-deranged, semi-oneiric figure of Eva.

Eva, a modest volume of 84 pages, was written in 1930, two years after the publication of Breton's *Nadja*. That work had fascinated Rosamel, according to his widow Thérèse. She has shown me his copy of the volume. A contemporary of the surrealists, Rosamel del Valle had already followed all their writings, which reached Santiago somewhat faster than North America.

Surrealist theories about living and writing have been based on the conciliation of contradictories of the real and the imagined, the dream and the wakeful state, life and death, past and future, the high and the low, as posited in Breton's Second Manifesto. But I must hasten to add that theory has been easier to come by than the praxis of such theory. The illustrations of theories have actually come off better in painting than in writing, which partially explains the greater success of surrealist art over surrealist writing. Many a surrealist text begins with the verbal harvest of automatic writing or with an account of the explosions of unexpected mysteries and encounters, only to end in a standard gothic structure with phantasms that remind us of nineteenth-century dream-possessed figures or ghosts. It is hard to identify a work that is totally surrealist, and we must put together gleanings to make an artificial composite of a surrealist vision. The work I have uncovered and translated here, *Eva y la Fuga*, is as close to being a totally surreal work as any other I know.

Beginning with Breton, the surrealists have presented lists of literary ancestors whose works have included narratives of dream and madness, from the eighteenth-century gothic to nineteenth-century writers such as Achim von Arnim, E. T. A. Hoffmann, Novalis, Gérard de Nerval, and Balzac (particularly in his novel *Louis Lambert*). They have not pointed out the distinctions between these filiated writings and their own: namely, that these earlier writers dealt with the irrational as a state quite separate from the rational, from what is explainable in rational terms. The irrational for these earlier writers was an aberration or a sublimation. When aroused by this state of the poet, the narrator was overwhelmed by distress or ecstasy. As in fits of madness or through a sense of epiphany, such states became signals of better things to come in an idealized supernal life or an inevitable descent into hell. The surrealists, by contrast, tried in their rational state of mind to induce the irrational functioning of the mind: to perpetuate the dream, to observe and enjoy with freedom and not with fear its impact on daily life, its transformation of standard rhetoric, and to perceive through these communicating vessels the fluctuations in the total composition of human experience.

The most celebrated heroine among those sparked by madness in surrealist writings has been Breton's Nadja. *Nadja*, Breton's best-known work, was classified as a "novel" against the author's will. Breton put his narrative in the form of an autobiographical text precisely because he thought of his random encounter as part of his daily existence and not as a fictitious account, and precisely to demonstrate that such a phenomenon can be a part of the life experience and not its opposite. Within the framework of his account of the life of a young man in Paris, apparently without a work routine, in the company of numerous friends, going to the theater, sitting at café tables, enjoying the kaleidoscope of the Paris scene, the encounter with the unusual Nadja is neither a divine bonus nor an act of damnation.

He meets her and tries to share her frame of mind and frame of reference. She heightens his experience in ordinary walks through Paris; she intensifies his natural visionary ability, so that at times he can share her less inhibited images of the real world—that is, what we consent to call the real world. He tries to idolize her (in Nerval fashion), but he cannot fall in love with her. Thereupon she disappears. Later, when he hears of her incarceration as a madwoman, he bemoans the fact that as a society we cannot cope with nonconformist behavior except by putting bonds on it. Though he has acquired a sense of freedom and broadened his field of awareness through her, he has not turned her away from any of her irrationality; in fact, his presence in her life has been a stimulus to aggravate what we would consent to call her mental imbalance. The relationship has changed both of them: she has gone off the deep end, he has let down inhibitive barriers. Nadja has been a medium in the deepest sense of the word, for through her he has proved his own theoretical hypothesis that one can abolish contradictions between the so-called rational and the so-called irrational.

Breton concluded *Nadja* with a sentence that was to

prove catching and catalytic: "Beauty must be convulsive or not at all." He characterizes as "convulsive" the effect Najda had on him. The involuntary, unexpected movement, by its power to astonish both its creator and its receiver, acts as an earthquake and moves one to action. Every surrealist after Breton had to come to grips with his own personal life: to determine how far he could prolong the dream that verges on insanity. But the Eva phenomenon did not apparently alter the exterior pattern of Rosamel del Valle's life.

In keeping with his habit of neglecting his own works, Rosamel never got around to publishing *Eva*, although it circulated among his friends. It was not until 1970 that, with the encouragement of his friend-poet, Juan Sánchez Peláez, an editor at Monte Ávila, it finally saw the light of day. Other posthumous publications have included another poetic narrative, *Elina Aroma Terrestre*, *Adios Enigma Tornasol* and a comprehensive anthology of his poetry. Several of his works— chronicles, diaries, literary and art criticism, and five stories titled *Esperame en Brooklyn* [wait for me in Brooklyn], all of New York vintage—still remain unpublished. I became aware of him and of the circle of his friends twenty years ago through Angel Flores, who introduced me to Thérèse. I visited Chile and have in the last few years attempted to translate this text, whose difficulty lies in the fact that it moves analogically from thought to thought and perception to perception, in a *clair-obscur* idiom that hides and reveals meaning at the same time.

The work is a first-person narrative about a haunting experience in which the interventions of the outside world are the emblems of an inner reality, awakened, pursued, lost but ever recuperable.

Such is Rosamel's presentation of the figure of Eva as a cross between a dream apparition and a real but deranged woman. She enters Rosamel's life "out of the blue," as the saying goes, but in this case it would be more appropriate to say "out of a circle of red."

> I meet her while looking at a coat of arms with strange colors—something between those that highlight black and of course red—and one on which could be read the inscription "Norwegian legion." Grasping Eva's hand, I can only exclaim:
> "My Eva, in the land of snow!"

Before the encounter he had prepared us for a dream and evoked her name, although he had not described her in any way in or out of dream. There is nothing metaphysical about this dream of an encounter with a sensual and at the same time ephemeral woman, dressed in red at their first meeting, and "surrounded by a red river and a frightful white wind." There is nothing abstract: the total experience is composed of physical sensations. The dream arises around and within the narrator like a tide, first to his knees, then up to his stomach, his chest, and his head. And there will be no solution either in escape with her or escape from her.

Whereas Breton's *Nadja* began with the question "Who am I?" Rosamel del Valle's running interrogation focuses on the identity of the Eva-persona who entered his life, capturing both his interiority and exteriority. It is by exploring *her* identity that he expects to understand his own. The flights and returns of Eva are depicted in terms of fugues, penetrating a circular rather than linear narrative without a beginning or an end, leaving the reader to dream of this *force*, the pursuer constantly changing places with the pursued, whispering in our ear that any ordinary encounter can become dangerous to our sanity. And if it does, it brings us all the closer to the poetic state, which is one of high risk.

Eva illustrates all the themes dear to the surrealists: the imaginary, the fantastic, the dream, madness. She is endowed with all these characteristics, but what is original in the literary context and in keeping with scientific knowledge of all these concepts is that instead of a bridge between the real and the dream, through her presence there occurs a *melding*, and we are never sure whether we are under the spell of the poet's extraordinary writing skills or witnessing a flesh-and-blood intimacy. In fact, in contrast to André Breton's relationship with Nadja, which is sexually discreet, Rosamel draws us into scenes of rapture with Eva. Appropriating the language of Claude Lévi-Strauss, we might say that if Nadja represents the aberrations of the *cuit* resulting from a superinvoluted, decadent society, in which a free spirit cannot function according to her nature, Eva is a primitive force—her name suggests it: the *cru*, the prerational surge rather than the postrational or antirational reaction. She absorbs sexual activity as a function whose justification needs no more debate than breathing or eating. The dream in which Eva comes to life not only is a state of subliminal beatitude in which every part of her body is worshiped but also, and often, consists of her accounts of brutal nightmares in which she is dismembered and made to bleed by lovers she has had prior to meeting the narrator.

We are not even sure whether the poet, in a spark of irrationality, encountered this girl roaming around the streets of Santiago bearing the evident marks of a prostitute, or whether she in her insanity accosted him and infected him with a touch of her irrational fever. Or perhaps, finally, the whole phenomenon is a figment of the poet's imagination at work projecting a dream figure—or inner model—for if he were an artist rather than a poet he might have made of Eva one of those fantastic figures like Giorgio De Chirico's or Salvador Dali's or Max Ernst's. But where Rosamel's figurative power comes most into play is in his ability to integrate the dream-figure into his humdrum reality. What makes me lean toward this last interpretation is the fact that there is no beginning or ending to the apparition of Eva in Rosamel's life. In Breton's *Nadja* the author casts this phenomenon into his autobiographical text and into his daily life, telling us exactly when and under what circumstances he encounters Nadja. He has the support of his companions as evidences of the reality of Nadja, and in a similarly authentic way he removes her from his life. Rosamel del Valle also evokes what he calls "the minor events of my life," but his companions seem as much dream-figures as Eva does. Like her, they appear unexpectedly and disappear in fade-outs as they might in a Buñuel dream sequence.

Rosamel repeatedly brings into question the authenticity of the character; although the encounters are projected into street scenes, home, amusement park, bars, and other familiar places, the poet suggests an eerie atmosphere (*clima* in Spanish) which is all his own, shared only with Eva. "Thanks to Eva's magic I am able to peer into the secret transformation of objects." She is constantly skirting oblivion, living at the edge of a precipice, and she draws him to the brink of the *pozo*: "I see nothingness quiver like a bough of ashes between my fingers," he remarks. Like Nadja, she is a *voyante*, a *vidente*; she is a medium, and, like Nadja, she reaches a zone of "maximum despair" where the pursuer cannot or dare not follow. But it is even more grave: she is nothing ("You, Eva, come closest to being what is not"), and at the same time she is everything, with a certain transparency and solubility that make her penetrate his things and his thoughts.

> I see her floating in a photograph, inside a thought,
> with eyes, mouth, hands, and feet like everybody else's.
> But more than anything else inside a thought. Why not

recognize her, now, in the desert, at the side of a well, leaning, contemplating herself in the water?

She comes to him "with reflections from the zone in which the senses multiply," and then the imprisoned self and the self that is supposed to be really himself "regain a single personality at the contact of love."

After giving us many premonitions that Eva's dark destiny will make her disappear forever, when she actually disappears in terms of the narrative's closure he does not know what has happened to her. One of his conjectures is that she has been confined to an insane asylum, as is the case with Nadja. And Rosamel's reaction to such a fate is, as in Breton's case, an attack on society's miscomprehension of the mind that is considered deranged because it can sense the rhythm of the universe and the simultaneity of time present, past, and future better than that which we call "normal."

In any case, her disappearance is not explained by death but by her having wandered off—we might say— on a wavelength that his antennae can no longer catch. He admits their ultimate incompatibility by saying that "your thought and mine bypass each other, though our hands are interlaced." She had come to him within an aura of the color red, and she disappears the same way. The well and the star with which Eva had been associated in each of her appearances are still present, but there is a ripple in the water, and it is encircled by an aureole of red.

> I like to believe that very close to me there is a ripple that could well be from a small well with a star at its edge. Again, and I believe for the last time, the color red. For this well lets us guess her presence through a red circle. It is the color of fire, of anguish, of bullets, of the only climate possible. The color into which Eva has fled as if rushing, perhaps, to the stake.
>
> Moreover, at this same hour and in a place that I do not seem to be able to identify, a flower is opening up

its black corolla. I can hardly hear the sound it is making. A weak fire sparks my suspicion that a flower without a name is growing not far from the "cry for help" area of my vital zones.

One of the tasks surrealists have found most difficult to suggest metaphorically to the reader is the point in time and space when a realistic activity skirts the unfathomable abyss. This point, as we have seen, Rosamel identifies as the "cry for help" zone. In Maurice Blanchot's *Thomas l'obscur* and in Julien Gracq's *Au Château d'Argol*, we have identical images of swimmers who move out to a certain point, distancing themselves from *terra firma*, and then have a compulsion to return. The normal and immediate reaction of the reader will not be one of surprise. He will think, of course, that as rational, practical creatures they know how much stamina they have and how much reserve to get back. Doesn't every swimmer have that experience? But in both cases *au large* means more than "swimming out"; we get swept into a metaphor that questions how much we can control and what can engulf our physical and mental powers into uncontrollable situations.

For one who has read surrealist fiction, it is therefore not surprising to recognize Eva as that kind of a swimmer: "I see her body like a swimmer's, her head, her heart entering perhaps into the magic circle of a dream." Sometimes the swimming figure "glides through the crowd." The other, more familiar surrealist attitude prominent here, as in Breton's tale, is the sense that both narrators convey of living like sentinels, on the alert—the "who goes there" of the sentinel's posture being a signal for the unexpected that occurs not on a stageset and announced to the reader by way of saying that we are in a dream world, or fairyland, or among the inmates of La Salpétrière, but within the framework of ordinary inhabitants of this planet going about our standard routine. To be a poet is to be a living seismograph detecting the slightest tremors of disruption of stasis, regularly skirting a well that might be simply an abandoned pit or might suddenly bubble and pour out fuel for a dream. Or we may be appraising dead wood that suddenly kindles, or we have stirred up a swarm of spiders or fireflies that seem as if they will never be exhausted. For the person always on the alert, a tour of Luna Park, where thousands of people are enjoying the normal sense of excitement and chatting of daily matters, will be a vertiginous experience; the poet Rosamel, with his dream/madwoman Eva at his side, will suddenly be subjected to the music of the spheres, the cataclysmic movement of the earth, and illuminations that exceed the lights of the amusement park.

Breton allowed Nadja to speak very minimally; much of the language he put into her mouth is a *metalanguage*. Eva, on the contrary, is extremely voluble, and in her discourse real-life incidents and visionary images are so mingled that one cannot split them into separate classifications. As she narrates her past life, Eva describes flights into the countryside like the vision of hotels in Valparaíso, a seaside resort near Santiago. She tells stories of sexual initiation, mistaken identity, brutal lovers, all in the condensed language of dreams, divested of the sense of time. The metaphoric structure is very closely related to folk culture and to the chthonian manifestations of nature in which Eva is deeply involved. Rosamel is a match for her: he sees her perched on top of trees, surrounded by butterflies that spill gold on her skirt—"everything is Eva." She is for him, as he remarks, "what is deepest in my dreams." When she vanishes, he is abandoned to "the great waterless night of the void." Sometimes it is not Eva but the others who vanish, creating a mental desert in which Eva and the poet interact. In these self-created realities there occurs a sudden vacating of crowded areas of urban comings and goings, whether in the presence of the great Ferris wheel in Luna Park or of the towers of the Iglesia de los Sacramentinos. The passage from the familiar to the unfamiliar leaves the couple in an open-ended space reminiscent of De Chirico's *Mystery and Melancholy of a Street*, to which the poet alludes at one point. The successive encounters, despite their recognizable landmark features, are transformed into a self-made cosmos, and recurring evocations of the image of the pit or the well bear the reflections of human despair and the echoes of a cry for help. The paths taken are not only the streets of Santiago but also the erotic trails of Eva's dream body, sensual and spiritual at the same time. As a lover, the poet infiltrates her being, penetrates under her skin in a trance that combines the erotic with the oneiric.

Breton had tried and failed to love Nadja, although he was intrigued and excited by her in their fortuitous meetings. She became the blue wind that passed ever so gently over his destiny, causing a release from inhibitions and a swerve in direction. If Breton could follow Nadja only to a certain point, Rosamel surrenders completely to Eva; she is that mingling of radiance and physical necessity which he recognizes as love. But since Eva is characterized as an elemental force and love is a concept of civilized beings, it is she who does not understand the notion of love. Nadja served as a springboard for Breton's creative imagination; the same catalytic power much more certainly pushed Rosamel to the brink of the unfathomable, and he succumbed more totally to the seduction of the irrational forces within his own being, even as he conveyed the *in extremis* condition of the Eva figure by repeatedly associating the color red with her compulsion for self-immolation.

The alternative to the Eva experience is art. And Rosamel del Valle cites Freud in support of that alternative as he envisages it: "Only in art is it still possible for a man driven by desires to do something that brings satisfaction." This is the *récit* not of a young man in search of his soul but of one trying to capture and share the throes of process in the creation of poetic discourse out of the forces of the dream. The unique quality of the book lies in the fact that the writer in his double function as poet and lover is accessible at any moment, without due notice, to the oneiro-erotica, to which he offers no resistance; yet as a poet he is ever in command of the caldron of his poetic vision. In line with the surrealist propositions that life itself is the ultimate poem—container and contained—and that the written work is the spillover (*débordement*) of the poetic experience, the literary becomes a consequence of the existential. For Rosamel del Valle, poetry and love are parallel pursuits, products of the same soil. His ultimate characterization of Eva's existence is that it somewhat resembles the land whence it is possible that poetry derives.

At the end of *Nadja*, when Breton addresses himself to a new woman, unidentified, the reader is left to speculate on what will happen next to the modern combination of Don Juan and Percival. Love and metaphysical quest are integrally involved in his case, and release is only a preamble to reengagement. In *Eva* there can be no sequel, because what happens is cyclical and not linear. The poetry that has been created emerges from the climate that Eva has produced, and the climate survives beyond the real or imaginary existence of Eva because it has been amalgamated into the poetry itself:

> Supposing that the sometimes ambiguous existence of Eva had some relation to something that is happening in me—like the urge to write a book, for instance: one would have to admit that chance has made us victims of one of its singular games. But the apparent vagueness that resides in each act and even in each impulsive reflex of Eva does not stop having some

point of contact with the arcana in which my being
enters moments before working on the facts and the
language of that life that is not totally subterranean,
that flows from the passage of Eva at my side, as does
the desire to fill these pages.

In the thirty-five years that remained to his life,
Rosamel del Valle was able to keep a balance between
the Eva image and the routine life he led. There is no
reference to Eva in the rest of his writings, but some of
the most striking imagery in this prose that is really poetry is retained and repeated in other contexts. The pri-
mary images of this text—the pit, the star, the
sunflower, the enigma lying hidden in the natural
world of flying creatures—maintain what he had considered in *Eva* the "possibility of a permanent
subdream." *Eva* was a matrix text from which much of
his later poetry sprang. It may be significant that he
withheld from public revelation the outwardly calm
pool of which time after time he recorded the ripples in
his subsequent writings. Had he not said at the end of
his dream narrative, "Surely her warmth lingers on"?

His poetry emerged from that climate that Eva had
produced, and the climate survives beyond the real or
imaginary existence of Eva because it has been amalgamated into the poetry itself. In his many articles on
poetry, Rosamel del Valle describes the poetic state
much in the same way as he wrote of his contact with
Eva: "Now and forever the illusion." To love and violate
language is the poetic act.

Despite certain differences of focus, *Nadja* and *Eva*
belong to the same matrix. In the convulsive beauty
suggested by the quasi-madness of the two heroines the
poet in each case senses a vicarious liberation—
paradoxically, at the very moment when the propaga-
tors of that sense of liberation are running the risk of
captivity. In each case, the poet's protest against incarceration is in behalf not only of those classified as in-

sane but also of those encompassed in the larger metaphor of the human prison in general, familiar to all who reflect on the human condition. Whether the random encounter occurs in the context of waking reality or within the texture of the dream, its power disturbs the apparent immobility of the human psyche and expands human space. Desire takes many forms in surrealism, as its investigators know; the only sin is stasis.

A final word about the nature of the problems of translation. We have to follow the poet through the labyrinthine meanderings of complicated sentence structures, dominated by an ever-recurring present tense that gives a sense of the immediacy of apparition and dream within the province of landmarks of tangible reality. Although surrealists have long known and pursued the power of the dream, rarely has its omnipresence been so vividly and sometimes fearfully relayed as in Rosamel del Valle's superimposition of dreamtime upon narrative sequence, achieved by the persistent use of a present tense rather awkward to translate into English. Often where a past tense might have been more comfortable to the reader of English I have risked the use of the present, in order to give a sense of the immanence of life and event that Rosamel del Valle wanted to convey. Another linguistic shock that the reader faces in reading the Spanish, one that I wanted to preserve for the reader of the text in English, is the tricky process by which the narrator says one thing and immediately—in the same sentence—turns around and says the opposite, invalidating his first statement.

Other translation questions are of an ontological nature and inherent to the transfer of meaning from Latin-based languages to English. Latin-rooted substantives often contain a monistic union of concrete and abstract significations, particularly useful to the physical approach to spiritual problems which is so integral to the concept of surrealism. There are a number of these key words in *Eva y la fuga* which would be easy to convey without interpretation or paraphrase in French, Italian, and probably Romanian, but which in English need several substitutes to carry over the total meaning. Such is the repetitive use of the word *consciencia*, which becomes in the course of the work *awareness* and *knowledge* and reaches out toward the recognition of phenomena that skirt the unknowable and are as ephemeral as recognition of dream-existence. How much easier would be the translation into the French *conscience*, with its parallel load of ambiguity! The same kind of impasse occurs when one tries to convey the uncanny meanings that radiate from the recurring use of the word *salida*, which is *exit* and doubles for release both of a spiritual and a physical nature, and passage from the rational to the irrational. It is also an emergency exit, a way out of the rigidity of life, and is associated with a cry for help. And the *asfixia*, which transcends in meaning the sense of physical choking, is a traumatic symptom of the narrator's spiritual asthma, triggered by all the constrictions of life to which he is subjected each time he is deprived of the Eva-principle. The central image of the voyage into the unfathomable is a *well* with a star at its edge. But the Spanish word *pozo*, so easily conveyed as *puits* in French, seems to suggest simultaneously abysmal depth and an ever-replenishable source of water, conciliating thus the antithetical significations of life and death, of consciousness and oblivion. Finally, and most important, the *fuga* of the title and the leitmotif of the narrative can never be given a true and complete value in a single parallel word, because it means both fugue and flight, conveying both the musical sense of successive movements linked together and evasion in the sense of rupture from familiar reality into a sphere from which there can be no return. The epiphany thus created, which comes to a climax toward the end of the work, loses its hypnotic frenzy in English because of the impossibility of finding in translation one word with the two meanings. That is why I have used in the translation of the title the word "fugitive" with the root "fugue," rather than the more lexically parallel "flight."

Yet in spite of these frustrations I hope that enough of the meaning and the rhythm of *Eva y la fuga* will come across in this first translation to convey the unusual quality of this work, which in both its language and its spirit contains that exceptional combination of the earthy and the ethereal, the elemental and the subtle, for which the Spanish language, particularly in its Hispano-American permissiveness, is the enviable medium.

But enough of analysis! Let us now begin to listen to the voice of Rosamel del Valle as we plunge into his shockingly irrational introduction, which instills the uncanny *clima* of a world in which the dream moves freely in and out of human consciousness through the interstices of sleep and waking.

ANNA BALAKIAN

E V A
THE FUGITIVE

*. . .Because all around me
there is something whose beat is a persistent
idea about to explode as my detection takes me
through the first gates of a sense of great panic,
an almost indestructible layer of foam that is
not, as one might expect, a barrier but the very
passageway, unavoidable though difficult of access. I am approaching this conniving thing and
can distinguish nets and scents filling the air.
The idea moves so close to me that I feel it
stretching, resurging, wandering from one side to
the other, trampling, tiptoeing, and then heavily
snorting around the fire that for the moment re-
fuses to kindle. It appears that in being drawn
into this difficult commitment nothing of my
own true self is in danger of collapsing into dis-
solution. In fact, on this wall that is not totally
horrible I cast the reflection, cold and pallid, of
the flicker of illumination within me, of my reason that at all cost engages its total and inviola-
ble capacity. From now on there is no greater
pleasure for me than to struggle between the pull
of a hand hovering over nothingness and the
reassurance that there is a way out if I should
need one. For the time being I am quite satisfied
to lean my old head toward that glowing thing.
Surely the trauma caused by an unrelenting de-*

*bate over what is salvageable of my being can-
not continue forever and a day. But I haven't
the slightest idea what I would have to be or do
in a space where there would be few things in
need of explanation or in a land full of light
where one did not have to anguish over nothingness. Other than this dread of the void, what
else is there in this world? And to the easy routine of the lost and found I prefer the anguish of
the terrors that are visited on man when his being in a delirious trance turns into a more or
less floating corpse.*

*What extreme toils do these spiders under-
take; they become not only spoken words but
tongues around the fire, and what is the dream
that is hovering over them? And don't tell me
that one of these days they will give me a mental
breakdown, when already they represent an impending asphyxia. For otherwise they would not
be the unexpected but inflexible vehicle of
thoughts not yet wrenched from the abyss. From
all this we may infer that these thoughts are neither its personification nor its precise impact
but that they are at the very center of things, a
point as undesirable as it is unreachable. Therefore there is no problem in recognizing the im-
minence of this thing that with the best
conditioning of the world is preparing to enter at
last into the dream.*

*How can I accept even temporarily the har-
mony that is being offered to me like a pulver-
ized flower? I reach down under its corolla, and
the sulfur of its eyes is not so strong as the*

stench of a corpse being waved by a dreadful hand. A single glance and the foggy land is mine, the very one I had previously inhabited at the cost of terrible anguish and collapse. Its stream of smoke reached me as if it were the most natural thing in the world, and it couched my thought; what a strange thing to do in order to live at the edge of wells. What can one see inside? Those faint but beautiful reflections are the food that fortifies the best of my days and nourishes my knowledge of things. The waves I make with my hands and the foam that rises from my body will go in pursuit of the unseen, of the pale fever of a being in the darkness. Is that the source of this penetrating asphyxia that I did not know before?

Well, I have to admit the precipices of this dream are as human as any other, so full of dark solitudes and sensations, but there the statue of man is not made of dream or of stone but is responsive to deep calls not unrelated to great upheavals.

Must I stake my life to capture its earthly warmth?

Does man turn his back on his own memories?[1] Or perhaps the dawn came in heavier footsteps than usually, with something obscure in the dew or in the oscillations that space provides for it in such a splendid way. For at that moment the dream began to invade me from the tips of my toes to my knees. It was a precise and persistent weight. Now this atmosphere covered me more and more, rising to my stomach, my chest, my arms, and finally my head. The dream! How light I must have felt in that awakening, and what winds were blowing ever so lightly over the earth not yet totally risen out of darkness. However, before falling definitely into a beautiful state of asphyxiation, I could still see the dawn making its way through clanging noises into the world. I admired its gait, slow as a roaming death, its eerie joy, its face like an oversized and overbrilliant flower. Then a wind began to blow with heavy wings, and tall trees raised their luminous branches. What kind of a wind is this? And what is this atmosphere that grows pale, or shines, that grows and expands and then suddenly falls as if into an abyss? And this great and blurry countenance of things? I ask you, Eva. I ask myself and I ask your patiently wrought wisdom in the hard and soft flames of the dream. I ask, Eva. But in vain. No matter what, although this reality did not belong to me, I would still have questioned myself in this same manner before having chanced upon your existence, before the darkness of your destiny. Could it be that the star of your life dwelt in the woods or in some city that exists only in a dream?

Around noon I rush into the street like one blindly impelled by the dictates of his memory, and driven toward something or some point that could be called the irremediable. The Avenida España is shining like a bright eye. From far—from where? I catch sight of a woman dressed in red. The color red. I see a bridge on fire, swinging like a branch. The presence of red immediately evokes the idea of murder, or of flight. (Consequently, or as if to confirm this thought, the morning is letting blood in the four corners of the world.) Whatever the reason, the woman is Eva. I meet her while looking at a coat of arms with strange colors—something between those that highlight black and of course red—and one on which could be read the inscription "Norwegian legion." Grasping Eva's hand, I can only exclaim:

—My Eva, in the land of snow!

Actually, it is cold. And I must add that between her and the Norwegian coat of arms there is a red river and a frightening white wind. "A red river, a wind . . ." asks Eva, and I could see her face turning toward the land of snow and cloud and her hands weighing a thought not quite lucid and slightly convulsive. In fact, Eva impresses upon me the darkness of her destiny.

On our way to the center of the city, Eva tells

me the horrifying dream she had a few nights before. "I am going on a journey," she says, "and I
come upon a land of snow and cold. The trees are
swinging their feathery branches, and in the distance a river is carrying hundreds of snow-covered
boats. The boatsmen are singing, and their song
spreads over the river and reaches out toward the
towers of the port and toward the sea. For there is
a port"—needless to say, I follow Eva's story
literally—"and this port is in the form of an enor-
mous horseshoe made of snow. I come down to
earth. The song of the boatsmen continues to en-
gross me, and at times I seem almost to be hearing
bells. At the next street corner there is a tavern. I
enter and ask for something to drink. Suddenly I
spot a mirror. A woman alone at the bar. After a
while my mouth begins to feel parched. I notice
that alcohol quenches my thirst as much sometimes as, for example, a drug. Soon I am again in
the street. I hear footsteps behind me. A man is following me. He overtakes me. Without knowing
why, I am trying to escape. Impossible. Then my
life doubles like a thought." Eva stopped talking. It
even occurred to me that she really did not feel
like continuing her story. But a few minutes later
she informed me that the dream was starting
again. Then, it would seem, the man took her to a
hotel. He wanted nothing from her, absolutely
nothing. He had only one desire: to cut her up into
four pieces. And he did it with a smile, with extreme deliberation, and without the least terror.
"Oh!" said Eva, and I could not calm her down.
Oh, no, actually she was calm and even as I
thought, smiling: but as for me, my words were

collapsing, and the world was slipping from between my fingers like an echo. I could see Eva being destroyed, exhausted, bleeding on corals, red corals, red foam.

For the first time I understood that something was going to happen between Eva and me. At first it was like a clashing of two atmospheres. Or else—and I think that this thought may be more accurate—like attempting something that has never happened before—I felt as if I was walking among hundreds of passersby, one of whom was going to say to me suddenly: "Tomorrow the sky will depart." That's how life is, full of such sparks, even if we do not want to believe it. Does the eye, that anticipator of our days, open and close according to the highest voltage of the life process whose victims we may or may not be?

Our morning encounter ended in the Restaurant Martini. There I noticed that Eva was totally unaware of the people around us. I observed that her thought was wavering between strange sensations; in fact, I detected a definite anger that shaped (her lips looked as if they were about to bleed) into a tune from the *Persian Market*, I think—and something that seemed to me to become the reflection of herself; its meaning evaded me completely.

Two days later, and absolutely by chance, I encounter Eva crossing the arcade, Pasaje Matte, in obvious distress. When she sees me she stops short, surprised, as if I had caught her off guard, interrupted not her movement, nor her expectations, but a point in her thinking of which I was unaware. Then quickly she changes—that is to say, she makes her reentry into the world—and it is obvious that her trouble has left no mark on me, and that my words have not had the least desire to penetrate what may have been her secrets. We left the Pasaje, and I asked her to accompany me to a bookstore. A minute later I felt as if I were waiting for something or something were waiting for me, and it was as if Eva and this feeling had created an occult relationship that was of very special importance to me. Now back in the street, Eva lost her tranquillity again, as if it were impossible for her to cover up an act that might appear strange to me. As for me, I made her realize with total ease that unwittingly I might have been intruding in her affairs. When finally I found myself on firm ground, she took me by the hand and, in a voice full of despair, called me "her friend, etc." I was not surprised by anything except perhaps to see night rolling out of Eva's eyes.

Is it possible that in life there is, how shall I say it, no natural protection? Eva tells me little, since, at times, although she does not seek it, *she is subjected to certain things*, to "certain abysses," according to her expression. Possibly. I realize that this is the most anguished side of her existence. "Let us see, can a woman like me live forever honorably?" She constantly repeats this. To show her that I understand, I trace small symbols in the air with my hands. A little later, and oblivious to everything, Eva explains to me that she had thought of devoting the previous day—her birthday— totally to me, inasmuch as, she added, she was feeling less disturbed, but on the other hand she

preferred not to try to involve me in "situations."
(Does Eva realize that my life does not adjust well
to everything?) Having found no other way to
please her, I give up the idea of going to the bookstore and invite her to dinner instead. She begins
to make excuses, I cannot pinpoint the exact circumstances. In any case, I have a feeling that she
no longer wants to encroach on my freedom, my
habits, subjected as at that moment to an unexpected encounter. That is what I think I understand. Then, realizing that her words do not
succeed in clearly expressing her thought, she ends
up by accepting. Somewhat troubled, she takes my
hands again; it feels like a branch bending at the
water's edge or like the sudden apparition of a
nameless star.

Interpretations, Eva, I need interpretations.

ANOTHER HEAVY DAWN, a day with light wings. The
shadow diminishes until it is a dot neither on my
right nor on my left. I notice that the slightest
tremor of my memory leads me to conflicting positions or, for instance, to a spot where I distinguish only wet winds. Half asleep, and with great
difficulty, I question myself. There is a blue-and-
green ribbon that unfurls and probably represents
the flight of sound. Soon the color green disappears, is dissolved into fine sparks, and begins to
roll horizontally into a red ring. Again the color
red. I am driven by a violent need to disturb this
small visual phenomenon by means of certain verbal variations, obvious as they are: "There was a
time when I loved the cascades of the deep night,
all red, and a rain of fine angel blood. The color

red. The color of a heart in the throes of despair, and an empty hand that extinguishes death. And the red horses speed, tormented, across the sky. Until finally the ocean bleeds its foam, and boats come and go like those thoughts that have a way of haunting us and in whose presence we do not trust ourselves to set the empty page on fire. Surely we are living at the edge of a precipice. The frozen waters reflect our image like small dots that we are not willing to see completely, in places that we are not anxious to locate. It is toward these distant red spaces that we have to direct the best and worst in us. But we are afraid of the rather heavy windlash, the oozing blood; we fear the great red flower of possibilities. For once, my delirious reality is no more than a monologue rambling about a woman who has something to do with my existence and about a night when wine was the ultimate coral that my dream extracted from the brilliant heart of the sea."

At the peak of the brief delirium that managed to slip through my fingers in a very natural and precise manner, Eva bursts into my room along with the morning light. There may have been sunshine outside—as they say, brilliant sunshine—but my body is floating in a whirlpool that can hardly be distinguished from the dream. Eva is speaking, and I hear her as if someone were calling me from the bottom of a well or from the other side of a wall. Is it you, Eva? It is cold. This leaf that is moving so lightly in the void, is it your hand, Eva? Through you the snow falls on a land of music.

A few minutes pass and then Eva is really at my side, and we are talking at length about the preceding night. There is no doubt that we visited certain night spots where alcohol and music played overwhelming roles. But among certain things that Eva remembers a few are worth mentioning—for example, the agitated appearance of the Torre de los Diez in Santa Rosa Street; the statue of San Martín and its circus number; the Mapocho Station with its three closed eyelids; and the river that now is no more than the black Sena de Rocambole, and whose murmuring dream awakens in Eva a strange fire, or an impulse that drives her into one of the miserable corners— which one?—of her destiny.

But the memory of the night begins to take the shape of a small bonfire, around which our re-membrances become so audible that uncon-sciously she and I simultaneously recall certain experiences whose glow imposes what we com-monly call "the force of destiny." For Eva's dream principle is "I have seen a man who raised a burn-ing hand."

—Do you remember reading avidly one day this title of a four-column article in a periodical: "The Assassination of a Five-Year-Old Child?" Then, according to what you say, driven by a crazy impulse you were so overjoyed that something be-gan to sing within you. I can't forget the blood that flowed then from your hands like torrential water, nor the way in which, instants later, in despair, you seemed to ask yourself:

—Who can I be at such times?

—Was that not precisely what invaded you, ac-cording to your admission, once upon a time?

Eva's fire is rekindled: "It was Sunday"—she is

speaking again—"a day when we would suppose the streets to be full of people. Is the world expected to change its mood on a day like that? But that's not my problem. It was as if I were looking myself over. Suddenly a man appeared. You know the little game we play at such times. Then we wander along side by side, embarrassed by the situation. The sun set its warm foot upon us. That is to say, it was slowly descending into twilight. I must confess that at that time I was living quite marginally. Everything was marginal, do you understand what I mean? I was totally aware of what it means to walk, unexpectedly, on such and such a day, at the side of a man, that is to say of a perfect stranger.

"How did I enter the existence of that man? Later I thought about that. Naturally, and unlike women who walk the streets, I did not act like a future and hopeless captive, that is to say, unapproachable. On the contrary, a strange force drove me to rise, to be lifted out of myself in some way or other and at any cost. But do you ever get what you want? My man was not, it is true, what I had imagined, or let us say that he interpreted my behavior in his own fashion. Is it still possible to say of anyone that *he behaves like someone*? It was at that time, I must confess, that I had my first incident. Since then—that was eighteen years ago—I have never gone back to see him."

On my part, I agree with her that on that day she must have had her initiation to life. And that, henceforth, it is not hard for her to explain any inclination toward delirium, toward suffering from lack of fulfillment, despair over foolish love affairs.

In fact, it is on that level that the spirit of Eva attains the difficult relationships of the world of dreams. Therefore, it never seems strange to her to hear me constantly evoke situations in which she was unwittingly victimized, vivid scenes, in her own estimation, in the umbrage of a friend, and the statement enacted as "with her head in the air," permitting me to record this story as she spoke and spoke almost without emotion at my side. (I must confess, on the other hand, that I let myself be driven by a strange force and almost as if it were natural, since my thoughts were not even able to lift the fog of the previous night.)

Here we come to a kind of interlude:

"They are, Eva and he, in Valparaíso.[2] It is October, 1929. During the day everything seems normal for her. They walk along the port from one end of the pier to the other, and as if to fulfill an immense desire. Then, the sea begins to obsess them to such a degree that they finally try to evoke stories, not necessarily of shipwrecks but of apparitions on the high seas, total sentences come floating in the atmosphere, waves lost or intercepted, heads in sweet slumber gliding over the water, etc. But at night everything becomes clear to her. For example, the first night, Hotel A: you feel that something is choking you. You think that it is the sea. The truth of the matter is that you are too close to the sea, and its sound is like the dripping of water inside you as if you were a fish." Second night, Hotel B: far from the sea. "Going up the stairs you saw 'terrible things,' you heard words addressed to you, and only to you, words with hardly any feeling, but that you *did not deserve.*

Then you had a terrifying dream. Two men
dressed in green—why green?—have entered the
room. They have gone straight for him (the friend).
A few sparse words and they tossed him out over
the balcony. Then you realize that *you* are the victim, not he, but you wake up to find yourself
stretched out on the beach with a broken leg and
a deep wound in your breast. The blood flows on
the sand running toward the sea." Third night, Hotel C: "After dinner, several of the guests initiate a
game of poker. You and he retire in highest spirits
to your room at last. Nothing. At midnight you begin to get restless in bed. You speak convulsively
and feel like screaming, you clutch your breast.
You have dreamed that you were playing poker.
You bet heavily and are in a state of wild excitement. Luck is with you. You are holding in your
hand a pile of chips. Fifty thousand? One hundred
thousand? Suddenly there is an explosive 'Hands
up!' No one moves. A policeman moves toward
you and greets you with the most gracious kindness, and with the same kindness delivers you into
the hands of the other who has followed him, who
in turn delivers you to a third, and so successively
until a couple of handcuffs are put on you. You
wake up, and it is impossible for your companion
to bring you back to reality. You groan, you speak,
you cry, until at last you manage to fall asleep
again. You wake up at dawn and exclaim: 'I have
been arrested, oh!' Now it is broad daylight and
you can't stop repeating: 'If only this were not a
mere dream. . . .' " Fourth night: "Hotel D: again
at the seashore. You have gone to the movies."

Eva's voice fails. I hear her in the distance. And

yet her body is too near mine, and I see her close her eyes, preoccupied with herself. The room vanishes suddenly. No voice, no life. But suddenly Eva regains consciousness. "There are so many things," she says, coming to herself. Now I hear her and I understand that she would never tire of speaking out in such circumstances, that is to say, when her whole being tends to skirt oblivion. "Yes," I answer her. "Our reality is too small when we are not able to grasp it fully."

"We live in forgetfulness rather than with memories," she says. "How can we reject what guides us, what supports us, what, in a word, we really are? How I wish that you could know everything about certain days of my childhood. Why? What would be the use of it? I don't know. It could be that a certain period of life might be identical in everyone. But does one remember it in the same way?" A pause. During that pause I notice that her forehead is illuminated again and that her body is shaking. "My childhood, my youth . . . ," she exclaims. And then a story.

—One day, in . . . well, no matter where, I saw the snow falling like this, in flakes. Why snow? But no, that is not what matters. I was eight years old, and I had a friend. Of course, I don't know to what extent it is possible to be a friend at that age. I only remember that he did not lose the opportunity to express a feeling that, as I learned later, was akin to what we call love. I loved the snow. . . . That and the other, and at that age. And why not? The days passed so rapidly for us, then the night came and there was nothing more than a great despair that set in. Do you believe it? A childhood filled with despair? . . . (When I think of that now, from such a distance, I am afraid that was the moment when the star of my destiny changed its course.) But with the coming of day, our games began again, as did our joys, our expeditions across a world that was not the same for my friend as it was for me. I remember that at times he treated me like a grown-up—that is to say, with admiration. Other times, and very often, he would require me to stare at him for minutes on end. Why did he like to look into the depths of my eyes? What did he see there? It seems to me that he was obeying a whim, although not always—how can I be sure of my memory now—because perhaps—after that the world changed for me suddenly. At that time I was what is called a happy girl. My friend, on the other hand, began to show symptoms of a precocious and horrible melancholia; I must say that I have never again heard adults say certain things as he did. And in fact, perhaps this act of plunging, as it were, into my eyes was not his moment of greatest lucidity and happiness. But who is to say? The days passed, and the months as well. My friend was headed for an end most visibly identifiable as anguish. I was sure that although aware of what was happening I was powerless to change his course. This continued until one night of the following winter when he fled from the house. The following day his body was found on the railroad tracks. His body, like a red flower on the snow. . . .

Now she is tired again. Now between Eva and myself there no longer exists any sort of absence. There is a road that begins and ends at the same point. This was so true that when she was overcome again by sleep I let her speak to herself, and her voice reached me as if from a distant point of the earth. Soon, it appears to me that I can see her leafing through some books and magazines, and I have an exact record of the admiration and disapproval with which she discovers some photographs or how she grapples for unimportant things, until she opens her eyes wide as she discovers in a book an engraving that represents a certain scene from the *Adventures of Telemachus*.[3] I hear her read out loud the entire chapter. And when she closes the book, much surprised by the condemnation of the kings to the punishments of a Tartar and "who were neither good nor bad," etc., a sudden "Oh!" makes her shut her eyelids and become so pale that I see her collapse with a sigh.

A little later on as we stepped out into the street, Eva repeated dreamily a poem that begins more or less like this:

> I see the day
> Only through my night
> It is a small soft noise
> From a land out of sight[4]

I understand once more that a human being consists of an infinite number of reflections. There is in you, Eva, a kind of "small, soft noise," which guides you, for instance, along a path that at certain hours, and often, as I suppose, leads you only into a labyrinth. Eva passes the better part of the rest of the day in a maze of poetry, which releases me from any need to comment on this fact. In any case, I could not help telling myself that a very shady tree was preventing me from seeing her entry into that death zone. And moreover, in the name of the most beautiful kind of despair I could not reject this thought.

CAN I GET ANYTHING else out of my existence with Eva? Ignacio Brandez brought up this subject. "You are depressed? You show that you are still trembling over what happened." We are together at the Bar Colón. But I have been thinking about Eva. Of the vanished Eva. I had lost sight of her for several days. "A wandering star," I said to myself, somewhat wistfully. But Ignacio Brandez laughed at me.

It is Christmas, and my friends are musing over bygone years.

—How can one forget them? And now we shall pass Christmas together again, as always, and forevermore. We shall remember that Christmas in Bar Alemán, the one at Estéfano's, one in the deserted room of our friend Samuel, at Irene's, and another one at Dr. Neuman's, the following one in that old living room, Centennial style, of businessman Montenegro, and the very last one at the recently vanished "Vaca Azul"—and so it went on.

But I can hardly hear Ignacio Brandez. And as a matter of fact, I am slowly beginning to lean toward a dream in which I see the body of Eva laid out in space. Her body floating like a bloodless hand. And in truth I see her surrounded by wreaths, all decked out, white, and yet she is murmuring. Judging from the blue stream of air coming out of her mouth, I believed her to be sleeping. Soon it was daybreak. And I could see space quivering like a bough of ashes between my fingers.

Eva! Eva! I know somehow that you are somewhere with hands falling and eyes fixed upon a space that is not this space but where your life is in pursuit of itself in vain.

I see her body like a swimmer's, her head, her heart entering perhaps into the magic circle of a dream, where she is joined by wonderful friends, with cherished things, where questions have returned and she sees their answers clearly written in the air. She seems more beautiful—if that is possible—and converses and joins at times in the music of the birds. Then she leaves the street, and the crowd lets her pass through in the midst of beautiful songs. Eva glides through the crowd and a dove alights on her shoulder, and the night falls upon the heart of the world.

This sudden invasion of images makes me understand once more Eva's valuable help; through her my memory is better able to grasp the meaning of certain thoughts or of certain experiences that reside in me day and night and whose signs, without her, would not be totally clear. Again that same memory through which I have had close knowledge of certain spaces where my being reaches the foot of certain walls against which I knock in vain! Anyway, there are certain walls on which I see clear imprints of my friends, those who hold no doubt the foremost positions in my memory. The simple roll call of their names makes me think of a small town where I walk the streets as a transient, as if in the trance of a somnambulist. Not far from these walls are others, especially one on which Eva's hand, with a handwriting looking like waves, has traced her name: EVA.

And, indeed with a flourish, a flower. A flower without color but distinct, making one think of the possibility of lying upon fire, upon feathers, upon thorns, and of not having to fall into any determinable place, and it is as if we were to say: "Life upon a breath." Had I not discovered this name and this signature, which is like a key, it would have been impossible for me to penetrate one of the secrets of Eva's passage through our world or to reject any kind of resemblance to certain wandering souls.

But Ignacio Brandez is, for the time being, life itself. His dark face, his black whiskers, the penetrating look are here, at my side, dropping certain enchanting words that only gnomes are known to possess. I see him smile and knock down the asphyxiated among the plants that my extended hand cannot reach.

—Your Eva, always your Eva, he exclaims, filling the glasses and surrounding me with smoke. But he does not pursue the matter.

Sometimes I see him enter my room, and his small beard darkens the world for an instant as if to cleanse it then and there and to show me its transformation. Around him I recognize those marine roots that sway in water and are like a dream. Thanks to Eva's magic I am able to peer into the secret transformation of objects, those that are living, like us, in a space where they become honorable people, where they greet us, can sit down and converse. I have seen them cross their legs by the fire, uncross them, separate them, and suddenly start telling stories about human beings whom they serve, for whom they care, and whom they like or dislike. For them causes and effects are identical, such as constant despair. One day, there comes a man or a woman, and seeing these objects ever so calm in the static character of their lives, these humans recover something of what they had lost of themselves, and they contemplate the objects, they dust them, they caress them, they move them around, and they make them believe that they alone preserve something like an invulnerable loyalty. That is love. Another day, a man or woman approaches them suddenly, and in their sweet solitude they realize that the living world is too hostile to them; that the prowling enemy is reflected in everything; that it is impossible to hide thought from witnesses; that still-life can also become anguished. It is then that things plunge to the bottom of wardrobes, of drawers, into deep corners, or crash to the floor. And that too is love. Only for them are cause and effect the same thing. They alone know that a human being is weak, variable, small, and useless. And no one dares abandon them for good.

But in all this world of things and in something that inhabits the mind of Ignacio Brandez, there is also room for human hope. Coincidentally with Eva's disappearances, her presence has been able to direct me toward the superspace whose keys are in her possession. It is not strange that in the company of Eva I have been able to find myself at the foot of the tree that produces the rainbow. And if my gaze follows the road that rises from the West, I spot her perched on certain treetops searching for nests. She is pleasurably surrounded with certain glowworms, with certain fireflies, with certain butterflies that spill their gold upon her skirt. The wind slips from branch to branch, from leaf to leaf, and at times holds in space insects that are sensationally ignited. And everything is Eva. There is a breath on her lips which is surely the breath of roots that warm the subsoil with a long and solitary respiration. That is why her head is surrounded with a halo that shines in the form of icons. Her feet, which hardly touch the ground, shelter the ants. And her hands, falling slowly to the sides of her body down to her thighs, make us believe in the existence of two small flowers without stems. As nothing disturbs her, I am terrified at the thought that there is a crushed star at the bottom of what she sees. That is one of the many allegories with which the presence of Ignacio Brandez brings me closer to Eva, who, according to him, disappeared in order to live.

After such a long, image-laden conversation, Ignacio Brandez puts out the smoke of his pipe with his hands and takes leave of me.

THE NEXT DAY, EVA. I was preparing to join Ignacio Brandez as agreed. But, as I must confess, what is the world for me without Eva? This uneasy feeling was often to return to me from now on.

After a few sentences whose content it is easy to guess, Eva draws me into the streets. This time we are going to Luna Park.[5] Christmas night is compulsively starlit; people go up and down the brilliant and monstrous Wheel as in dreams, and as if to collect the thoughts that are ejected from joyous minds or from those who are frightened by the circular ascension. I notice that nothing of all this is unfamiliar to Eva, and that her entire existence has been something like this, similar to the rise and fall of a Ferris Wheel. The blasting and persistent music of the pianola keeps reminding me of the music that, without being loud or obsessive, is connected with the things that surround her—that are likely to surround her forever—the things that make up her halo, perhaps. It is from that day on and with that thought that I can account for the secret bond that exists between her invisible human radiance and the living testimony of actions that would never have occurred if it were not for the power of attraction exerted by her passage. Eva smiles almost insanely when the Wheel begins to move. And she is suddenly silent when, now at the point of top speed, people's faces are illuminated there on the very top, and their eyes believe that they are at last crossing the threshold of heaven. The vertigo that at such moments makes their breathing rather heavy, and the panic that seizes them by the shoulder, is reflected in their faces like the shadow of the clouds upon the arena. Eva presses her arm against mine, but I do not feel the pressure, because between her eyelids and her mouth a desert stretches forth with an oasis of three trees and a well. In the distance, a caravan with slow black horses is raising something like white smoke, which remains floating for a long time in the atmosphere. For in the desert everything is white, and its soil exists only in dreams. The three trees cast their shadow upon the well, and I see her leaning over its edge and contemplating herself in the water, which is none other than the water of our dreams. As she appears suddenly in the solitude of the sands, there is nothing about her that suggests the shape in which she entered my life, filled the emptiness of my hearth, and then abandoned the obscure city of my body. Nothing gives me any idea of her shape, the shape that is lost and reappears. But I see her floating in a photograph, inside a thought, with eyes, mouth, hands, and feet like everyone else's. But more than anything else within a thought. Why not recognize her, now, in the desert, at the edge of a well, leaning, contemplating herself in the water? Why? When the pianola finally stops its music, Eva's arm really leans on mine. I see now the Wheel reject the people from its great musical and aerial bosom. I hear happy voices and words of relief and almost the kinds of remarks that suggest that they are ready to abandon it to its beautiful mirage.

We speak for a long time after that, although we hardly hear each other. But when the Wheel and its music are now far away, I feel the need for Eva's presence, to really speak to her, to be certain that Eva is herself and no other. But this is all useless. We are mingling with the crowds. We are carried away by the Christmas festivity. We meet couples, children, elders, people alone, soldiers, policemen. Pieces of conversation are blown into the air. "What are my chances of getting nabbed?" "Don't be stupid, old boy." "Here they come, Alicia!" "Look at that thing, what's its shape? It seems to be an egg." "It was impossible. Imagine, a friend, a pal, a drink, another drink." "Always you give me hope, Alfredo." "All this appears stupid to me. In my time . . ." "You are not a baby anymore, Lalo." "Mama, the wheel, the wheel!" "A

beer is nothing." "The English hour,[6] my life."
"Don't make a scene. When we get home I'll explain everything." "What friend are you talking
about?" "You must admire my character. How can
you want . . ." "Don't be a counterrevolutionary.
The party . . ." "Just the same there is poverty."
"This is not the right place." "Excuse me." "No,
don't be crazy. How can you ask that of me?" "It is
necessary. Don't cry. This will be our great night.
Shall we go?" "Good-bye, Bertha!" "The one with
the green dress." "The President." "The people an-
noy me." "How do you make out in roulette?" "Tomorrow at eight." "Does your husband know?"
"Nor see it." "Ten cents, ten cents. Who will not
give ten cents for a copper skeleton?" "I pay them
well, man. But they are communists. . . ." "No, no,
and no." "Now or never." "Think, think about it."
"Ten, ten, who will not give me ten for a skeleton
. . . ?" Voices, voices, but not Eva's. The asphyxiation lasted from the time we left Luna Park until
we were able to enter again into the darkness.
Then I heard Eva, and it was as if we were still before the Ferris Wheel.

—Do you notice? People look lost. Where are
they going?

The signal tower of the trolley looked as if it
had been set on fire there in the distance. The river
was running in a westerly direction, ever so nar-
row, ever toward the West.

—The poor are isolated. Here there are only
poor people.

I gripped her arm with force, agreeing with
what she had just said.

We cross the river. At one of the railings there

was a woman alone, leaning against it, with eyes fixed on the muddy waters, very muddy in the night. Suddenly Eva becomes alarmed.

—Like this woman I stood a whole night, she said, leaning against the railings of the Bridge of the Pyramids. Nothing happened to me, nor did I expect any ordinary thing to happen to me then. But I stood a long time refreshed by the water breeze. During that time I observed two things. A couple crossed the bridge. The man was angry. The woman, whimpering. They were having a discussion. I followed them. At the entrance of the Avenida de la Paz they stopped. The man called softly at a door. The woman seized his arm. She begged. She cried. The door opened, and I saw on the threshold another woman. The man entered. The one who was begging remained outside, left behind. Then she began to walk along a back street. Grief muffled her steps, blackened them in the night wind. I returned to the bridge. Suddenly there was a man there, a laborer. He passed by me without noticing me. From the other end of the bridge a policeman appeared. He stopped the worker. I heard him ask for something like his identification papers, or something else. The man made a move as if he could not comply with the request. Then the policeman took him by the arm. The man tried to cross the bridge again, but now he was arrested. At that very moment a tram passed. I took it. Inside, there were people going home or to someone else's house, totally indifferent yet surely happy.

—Her thoughts are traveling above the earth, tonight—I thought. And that was the wrong thought, I admit. For Eva's existence contains all the terrestrial warmth, and nothing is foreign to her, not even the magic of our reality. When she says "I see," she expresses what cannot be seen by simple sight. It is as if one were hearing a "there will be" or "and then." But the seeing state in her is like that of one in contact with a thought that is about to explode. Like herself and among all things. Thus, for example, in front of the Ferris Wheel she did nothing but let herself be driven by the forces of circumstance, while she was herself the circumstance. The desert, the trees, the well that I have been identifying with her strange absence are nothing but the living images of a reflection that appears frequently before me, and always when I am at her side. In her this reflection is life itself, the permanent reality, dream as beautiful as it is voracious.

—How can I hear her voice, then?

Perhaps Eva was silent, confirming the fact that this spectacle was controlled by nothing other than her mind, and thereby the joy or terror of the people became to her less anguished, more human, more like joy and terror. With her thought in action, the Wheel lost the sense of panic it created and could make people forget where they were going in the air, and as a result it made it easier for them to enjoy the sudden appearance and disappearance, for example, of the top of the Cerro San Cristóbal, of the crowded party, of the skyscrapers in construction or the towers from which come forth in various streams the sounds of bells.

That night ended in a secret place, and such an enchanting one, and nothing compels me to dwell on its details.

THE TRUTH OF THE matter is that at times I cannot explain to myself exactly how Eva remains at the core of a certain zone, how she is the wandering star that does not cease to run in this or that direction, but that I cannot stop seeing or admiring, and whose radiance never dims. It is only through her that I understand that star to be the level of being that, from a distant dream[7] to those days with Eva, is ever running toward a point where my destiny seems to be revealed with total clarity. For I see Eva in no other way around me, for example, doing hastily what she has to do, fearing to lose that time, which belonging to her must not be allowed to pass without reawakening the secret that she alone knows; and without its magic she would be unable to see or attain anything.

—What does she seem to be waiting for each day?

It would not be difficult for me to realize that nothing that happens to her occurs suddenly, and in that way the pace of her despair doubles. And so, one day when as usual she is on her way to La Plaza Brasil, a few steps from her destination she meets a friend of mine, the Señora B., who recognizes her, and is so surprised to see Eva in a place where she herself is in the habit of spending a few moments each afternoon and where she had never met her before that she looks down on the grass where her children are playing and suddenly sees a bleeding face floating in space.

—How crazy I am, Eva, Señora B. said to her, and she hastened to greet her, of course, and tried not to show the surprise or the vision that preceded her arrival. But hours later, in fact on my return home, I got the news that the husband of

Señora B., a friend of mine, had just died, having been run over by an automobile.

I don't want to belabor a point that Eva would take as bad faith, although it drives me into a series of contradictions and coincidences that seem to rise out of Eva's breathing. It has nothing to do with portents or witches. Here, as elsewhere, I must point out that whatever contacts Eva has with activities that lie outside the commonplace and betray her special secret entrance into things is unconscious, as is her invisible passage when there are moments of human stress. Besides, why should I deny that she may be the image of what lies deepest in my dreams, crossing my mind from time to time and never completely perishing? The undeniable fact is that her existence has established for me *a contact*. My being moved around this contact for a while like a fish in water. What seems to be my solitude was filled with movement. What I was and what I felt matched exactly the image and semblance of this contact. How can you resist opening your doors, one fine day, to a head so radiant, and how can you resist offering your bed to a body on the verge of collapse?

How can I say now that all this has nothing to do with life? For in truth at this very moment, when my thoughts are shrouded in a cloud, and which in spite of everything makes the things around me transparent, I hear Life, that is to say Eva, enter my home darkly dressed, a bit adorned with the distinct features of the dream. She stops a moment before the *Naturaleza muerta*[8] of Julio Ortiz de Zarate, where there are two dahlias time-filled with blood. Then, with what must be her power to stare, she looks toward the window, where the light of the setting sun is almost blinding. It seems to me that her thought casts a green glow on the windowpanes, and then I have to admit that she suddenly goes out into the street and gets lost in the crowd. As in *The Man of the Crowd* of Edgar Allan Poe, I feel that someone is calling me from afar, and that I must heed that call. And I run in pursuit, in pursuit of a *thought*. It crosses street after street. It is only on reaching the Avenida de las Delicias that it slackens its pace. Now it seems to be walking over garlands toward the Flower Market,[9] beyond which rises the tower of San Francisco Church. A new stop among the flower shops, where I observe that she is admiring the dahlias—it becomes the thought of a thought— which should have been arranged by Julio Ortiz de Zarate.

The pursuit ends a little farther on, at the foot of Cerro Santa Lucía; in its beautiful woods visible and invisible beings enter, and depart, some alone, others holding hands.

—Eva, Eva! Where are you at such times?

How terrible it would be for me to realize that the noise that pursues me is produced by the things that some day will finally build for me the city of oblivion.

THE PAINTING OF Brandez and the music of Estéfano are always entering arm in arm into my existence. And everything that has to do with it is taken over by the painting bugs and the music bugs. Ignacio Brandez gives me the secret, the color and the volume of a space where what exists in the least is the word "infinite." And Estéfano Lombes delivers to me the keys to its seven doors. What strange quiver do I detect in the slight movements of the sand, the fish, the stifling plants? There is, for instance, a turf and a white horse that comes to visit. The suboceanic air unfolds foliage of loose hair, and the corals wave silent horse-manes and packages preparing for the arrival of the fantastic terrestrial host. When silence returns, I find myself in a spot where nothing can be seen but from which it is easy to hear the visitor sleeping, with a smile, upon the turf.

Estéfano's face is not as clear in my mind's eye as Brandez's. I only recognize it each time that I see it with its big eyes fixed on me. His cleanshaven and somewhat melancholy face reminds me of those pale servants in English novels. His gait is firm, his head high, his hands behind him, as he stares fixedly at a spot that must surely be subterranean. And with it all there is his music. His *Caballo durmiendo en el césped* [the horse sleeping on the turf] lives within me like a column.

Behind it—could it be otherwise?—I recognize Eva's voice and the early sun that encircles her. In the afternoon, when the shadows begin to blur the appearance of things, there is a song. A ewe and a star dressed in green greet each other in the twilight.

Estéfano Lombes's hand is not a hand, it is a leaf. I squeeze it in mine, and yet his blood does not acknowledge me either.

—Eva's recent absence has driven me to seek out Estéfano now, I say to myself.

And in truth, he looks rather happy, and for the first time I see him smile as he embraces me.[10] Of course I am surprised not to have immediately noticed the dove that has just alighted on his shoulder. It is a bluish dove, and its eyes are burning as they gaze without being startled by anything, not by the dwelling that in fact is not a branch, not by the dance steps that make its owner sway, nor by my surprise as I observe it. The plumed creature is young, as far as I can judge. Estéfano enchants doves instead of serpents, something much more difficult. I offer a cigarette to Estéfano and another to the dove. I ask if they would like a *pisco*[11] with crackers. Estéfano accepts, so does the dove. Suddenly Estéfano falls silent, in ecstasy, his hands falling to his sides. And so speaks the dove:

"My former master and I lived in a section of Santa Rosa Street. My master made dolls. You should have seen with what patience his hands worked with wood, with plaster, with wax, with cardboard, with fabrics, etc. Mornings he stayed alone, then I roved in the arcade and over the neighboring rooftops and in the street. But in the afternoons he let me walk back and forth between the dolls. (There was something that appealed to my feminine sensitivity.) We were friends, no question about that. And my existence meant so much to my friend that the relationship bordered on love. But happiness does not last, as the saying goes. One day I perched long moments on the windowsill. From the next-door apartment something emerged that I could hardly recognize: there was a definite rustling as I had sometimes heard in the treetops, in the water, or in the electric wires.

Something there was that entered my ears and my plumage and was like a dust difficult to shake off. From then on, each day I closed my eyes in anticipation of that sound, which, as I have recently learned, is music. On the third day or the fourth, a hand reached out to the window. It wanted to catch me. And I ran in the direction of the area where my friend created dolls. The fifth day I saw the man with the sound effects enter the house. It was Estéfano." The pronunciation of this name was like the cooing of doves. "The maker of the dolls and the visitor became friends. From then on there were daily visits. My master, or my friend, thought that the visitor came really to admire his dolls. But how was I to know that he really came for me? And I, well, one morning, at dawn, two hands gripped the neck of the god of the dolls. And the assassin pressed me against his chest with care, as if I were a flower.[12] Now I understand that I did not have the same destiny as so many others, like those that have the form of a rag doll or are made of wax or wood. . . ."

When the dove called, Estéfano spoke. That is to say, really, the assassin spoke. His voice was a hollow sound that crashed like a furious butterfly on the windowpane. I recognized it as the voice of love.

—Is this not, Eva, the story of the bluish dove with which you so often softly converse in Estéfano's house? Now, and in homage to the summer that is coming, my friend has brought it back for a visit. And you are not here.

I HAVE JUST RECEIVED two letters, one from Pablo Neruda[13] and the other from H. Díaz Casanueva.[14]

Suddenly I remember that yesterday, while Eva was examining the lines of my hand, I heard her say in a most absentminded tone:

—I see three lines converging to a point. Among other things, it is like saying that in two faraway countries—one farther than the other[15]— there are two persons who are often in your thoughts. And the third line is that of infinity.

All right, Eva, I am sorry that you are not here with me right now. Here are the two lines. And the other? It is with some trepidation that I think of an existence determined by this red triangle.

—AND THE OTHER is infinity.

I admire the curious cults that Eva practices, extremely primitive cults, and it would be virtually impossible to argue with her about interpretations of them. Just as I have admired more than once the photographic reproduction of De Chirico's painting, *Melancholy and Mystery of a Street*,[16] I was amazed when passing one afternoon through Avenida Francia, Eva stopped short and looked toward the sky on the horizon where, at about the level of the hills, the new moon had risen. Hastily then Eva took from her pocketbook a bill and held it up.[17]

—For good luck, she says, and makes a wish or places an entreaty in the dark recesses of my hands.

Well, through the penetrating power of vision she handles the omen as an ambiguous message like those that a *voyante* of Nataniel Street offers in interpreting the apparition of a card preceded by the ace of clubs. "No, that is false," she said, and she snatched the card from her. I observed the stupor with which the *voyante* stared at the cards offered by Eva's hand and from which, two at a time, she extracted once more, a sure secret from the future. This scene made me admire for the first time the faith of the possessed and the overwhelming submission with which the women of Chile and of the world accede to the power that makes one cry out for the presence of something, the proximity of a radiance, whether it be of hope or of death. I maintain my stand against the rigidity of certain principles, especially relating to life, or better still to the pleasure or to the anguish of living. I have an intense hatred for everything that does not contain some secret exit, something like a secret passage leading to a *living void*. That is to say, I love the act of breaking the seal of that living void that justifies or sacrifices an existence by consent.

On the other hand, this existence is crowded with devastating days in which I see Eva struggling beyond her capacity, possessed of a strong need to succumb to what she herself calls her "excesses." I have never seen a smile such as the one with which she questioned me:

—Which of the two? This one or that one?

With "this one" she indicates the way of the dream, of solitude, of anguish, of letting oneself be transported, ultimately to reach the entrance to a world of closed spaces. Whereas the other one—her smile and the sign of her hands in the air symbolize then a blue flower that could well be an intermittent dream of alcaloids—it was a refuge, a flight toward the reverse of her indispensable desires, a flight to the brink of madness, the inevitable precipice, etc. She questioned me when she discovered in me a vague desire to liberate her from a kind of net or to find for her a passage toward a less anguished state. Then I felt myself entering a zone of darkness. For I thought I heard more than one reference to her existence as being a voluntary flight toward the brilliant "seduction of the void." But I came out of that zone the very minute that Eva fixed on me her big eyes. Then, the world stopped and a wind—I could touch it with my fingers—blew away, one by one, the impenetrable layers in which, thanks to her, I seemed to see my thoughts eternalized. Eva was entering me, I thought. And in truth, her life unraveled in my memory and brought along its music. I felt her crossing the threshold where despair was lodged for a long time. A breath of cold air hit her full in the face, for I saw her paling. She advanced. The first branches shimmered along the shores of certain waters no less brilliant than frost. At times they led her to certain phantoms not unfamiliar to Eva. Then she smiled before certain plants with large, entwined leaves, which curiously resemble starfish. Eva is like a visitor who had stepped into my own mental forest, her fiery foot almost always cringing before the vileness of the earth. When at last Eva leaves me, my thoughts seal my lips and then I know the night, the great waterless night of the void.

—THIS ONE OR that one? I see with pleasure Eva, a little pale, within a place no less vaporously white. Her existence happens to be the source of the vapor and moves from one object to another wearily.

Her head is bent toward the ground, and in the distance one can hear the echo of her passage in the summer atmosphere. A heat—a heat that is not of this world—advances in waves and dims the honey-red glow of the day. What climate is this? I feel it radiating from her body as if it belonged to her by magic, as if even the slightest movement on her part could change the climate, change time, change things, all subjected to her own reality. I cannot help but admire this land that Eva creates with a wave of her hand and that, in despair, she fashions into her own likeness. Nothing prevents me from imagining the expansive dream in which she situates it, with what a prolonged summer she surrounds it. In the center of this image Eva is stretched out, vaporized, white. From her head emanates a halo of vapor that rises from one level to another. The trees and plants fold up into an asphyxiating summer dream.

Then the dream loses its course. Life comes in large gusts of air, and one is drawn into the dance. I see that her country is filled with fiery cities, large factories, trains in the throes of panic, streets teeming with people, etc. I see her pass with her head bowed, still in dreams, but attentive to a rhythm that possesses her. "Eva in life!" I exclaim. Her solitude is sustained by a useless and frightening radiance we associate with drugs. It is possible that until love returns . . . What can men do with an empty body? And she passes. Passes among people and things, withdrawn into herself.

—What power do my hands have against this or that?

I confess that I do not believe everything to be extremely and totally useless; but my desire is stymied when, respecting the free-spirited way in which Eva copes with things, I must let her go her random way like a frail branch floating aimlessly upon the water.

—In the first place, and above all, let there be no new obstacles because of me—I repeat this to myself each time that she catches me in the act of trying to penetrate the constant despair of her earthbound spirit.

And then with a smile:

—Just the same, I am not the epitome of contradictions . . . oh, but I am!

Two days later, to distract my attention a bit from the many things that, according to her, preoccupy me, and for the sake of her peace of mind and because of the things that from day to day happen to her when she is far from me, she confessed to me that she wished to break away from everything that surrounded her, except, naturally, from me.

—I know it, one cannot shape life to one's own taste. Yet is that what I wanted? To be at least able to choose? And after a minute she would say: This is not interesting. How dumb I am! I really came to tell you something that seemed to me amusing. Yesterday someone visited me. A lady like . . . Eva accompanied her words with a certain mimicry and for no other reason than to give me to understand that she was talking of a more or less elegant and stylish lady. "Well, for all appearances 'a lady.' As I turned away from her, without any sign of wanting to enter into conversation with her, she said to me:

—Go on! Don't you know me anymore? I am Lucía. . . .

—No, Señora, I answered, and please excuse me. There must be a mistake.

—But Eva, how is it possible?

Nothing. I went back in memory one, two, five, ten years. Nothing. I fell back into childhood as if into a river. Nothing. And my visitor followed with her big eyes fixed on me, astonished each time a little more because of my bad memory. Impossible.

—You must be mistaken, I said to her at last, firmly.

—You must excuse me, Señorita, she replied. Anyway, may I sit down for a minute?

—Of course.

And I drew up a chair for her. Can you imagine? A few minutes passed, long ones for me. Finally my visitor began to apologize.

—Once upon a time I had a friend, Eva Bayen. It seems she had not heard from her in the past five years. A short time ago, she said, she had caught sight of me in the street. She followed me. She managed to see me, in quick profile, and her heart had filled with joy! Eva Bayen! But she could not catch up with me. From a distance she had seen me enter my house. She had asked about me; the only thing she was able to find out for sure was that my name was Eva.

—The truth is, no, you are not Eva Bayen. Please forgive me. . . .

But she did not stop there. She remained seated a few more minutes, and I noticed that she was trying to make me like her at all costs. I felt that she misunderstood again the indifference with which I was listening to her. In spite of everything, you understand, I felt a strange compulsion to let her say whatever she wanted. It has been such a long time since I have heard around me a woman's voice, I thought. I am sure that this is not a feeling, at least an emotional one. No. I let her speak. . . . When, finally, I really paid attention to her chatter, I understood the futility of my feelings. She no longer mattered, nor did Eva, but only myself. She spoke to me as to a friend, she said that she wanted to do me good. She had guessed that I lived a lonely life. She presumed that life presented a thousand problems to good-looking young persons like myself, etc. Do you understand? She ended up by offering me her house and, by wanting me to agree to our being like two friends, to enter into a life with no problems. As she got up at last, I noted that she studied me from head to toe as if assessing the quality of a piece of merchandise. What do you do with people like that? Nothing, my friend. I showed her to the door with my finger, and she could not get over her shock when she heard me say with complete calm:

—There is no doubt, Señora, that you made a mistake. Good-bye!

And Eva laughed out loud, playing with my hands and obviously satisfied once more with her behavior.

You don't think, Eva, that there is any possible release for your existence. Every exit door opens upon your own self.

Is it Eva and not a shadow of her passage that crosses my nocturnal city? But she thinks she is walking at a certain distance from where my thoughts are and, according to her own admission, imagines that my presence in what she herself calls her "impossible trances" is nothing more than the despair of flight. Then, she says, she runs to meet me, with never a thought that she might be abandoned, but with the fear—here her thought wavered—of not being always close enough to me. She does not want me to wonder for any reason, "What is happening to Eva at this hour?" "That is easy, a woman like me . . . and you would be right . . . or you would not be right." That is certainly the reason I meet her only once in a while in places where I would never expect to find her. And each time I observe that without appearing to be disturbed at being taken by surprise, she justifies her presence in such places in a singularly absent-minded way. I was, therefore, not surprised to see her one afternoon from afar, veiled in some kind of cloud, among suppliers of limestone who climb day and night inside the grounds of San Juan Hospital de Dios[18] in the Alameda de las Delicias. When I reached her she said to me:

—I came back to see the Torre de los Diez. It is pretty, even like this.

—And what's the idea?

I saw her hesitate a moment, as much as to say that such an idea did not warrant a firm and com-

plete admission on her part, above all when I enu-
merated for her one by one the people who take
this journey to perdition and among whom only
three out of all of them—Magallanes, Prado, and
D'Halmar—deserved (she singled them out, as-
suredly by intuition) in her opinion to be called
mad. And she agreed:

"The idea? After all," and, much later, emphat-
ically, "I do not believe in those roads that lead to
a little bit of infinity." And forgetting the idea, she
came to fix her eyes again on those live flames that
emitted soundwaves toward the sky.

During that day and various others I observed
that it is possible for Eva to live absolutely outside
herself. In the way she thinks about certain things,
and in the horror with which she discovers certain
facts she manages to conceal from me her ill-fated
star. And the truth is that her awareness becomes
more and more intricate. She invents oceans and
vast ships of angels who overrun the world. Her
hand can create the darkest fantasy without any
outside intervention. Shattered one day that she
cannot forget, and wavering in the pursuit of all
the things that have no limit and, what's more, no
security, the anguish of her life—of her life that
was not managing to avoid the horrible presence
of people—she resists all escape into an existence
that does not admit the reality of her actions, rejects everything that enters into conventional pat-
terns, all of which, according to her own
expression, is nothing in the long run but subterranean putrefaction.

The easy mores or the dangers that unavoid-
ably surround a woman facing the world alone

do not enter in any way into Eva's concerns. That certain people count her among the worst kind of persons, and others pursue her as if she presented an opportunity for them has no meaning for her except perhaps as an indisputably natural impulse. Why? And her smile says that she is none of the things that the world thinks her to be, that in any case she would be something else in the same dubious way. And for the time being, not counting on any other outlet than through my "providential friendship," she runs to my side and can see that upon my breast in the end, and from time to time, her wandering soul can find some rest.

I hear her sleeping, her head resembling a slightly faded flower that the West wind has gently whipped with its feathers.

"No, Estéfano. Truth cannot consist of this knot that tightens or loosens around our neck from time to time. What color would white be, for example, seen from the point of view of the knot tightening or loosening? No, Estéfano. According to the most simple reality night can have only one color. And yet according to the most delirious reality, this knot is tightened, and the earth seems to lean toward a color that is not precisely that of night. That this metamorphosis enters into the sphere of phenomena, be it so. But that whatever goes into you along with the fear of being, and as such lucidly resembles or even represents the truth that can trigger that great cry for help identifiable with the sense of being human, seems to me to constitute an irreversible blindness." Thus it is to say, as if in fear, that he had thought to be answering a

letter, hardly conventional in content, in which
dear Estéfano Lombes had wished, in his fashion,
to *liberate* me from the horrible subterranean place
in which I have fallen. And why subterranean?
Never before had I come closer to the things that
I was seeking, and never had the reflection of anything such as the atmosphere of a woman, or of
love, entered more fully my body and everything
that surrounds me. I believe in the vigilance of certain flames, not extinguishable at will, whose
flicker gives man a sense of truth, the true image
of what occurs at all hours in his terrified consciousness.

At this very hour I see Eva—"the fugitive," according to Estéfano, using the musical expression
of fugue, which is of course like her own nature—
lying in my bed as upon a bed of roses. Her arms
open wide, and my mouth travels over the paths of
her body, one by one, the streets that I become the
last in the world to walk through. Her head palpitates as if a tempest had passed over her hair,
over her hair that looks like honey, because it falls
all aglitter. Of course her mouth breathes dreams,
and I listen to her. Then I understand once more
that writing has nothing to do with love, nor is
sleep a drama for two bodies in embrace. For in
this atmosphere time does not seem to exist, nor
does indeed whatever follows enter into the curious seduction of time. Then, on Eva's neck my
mouth learns at last how statues breathe. But it is
in the area around her breast that I am overwhelmed by her breath. In this part of her domin-
ion I am not quite at home, and I see her as a little
while ago, on a bed of roses. At the point of separation of her limbs my mouth goes wild—even as

human existence wavers between two roads to explore, to the right or to the left. By which of the two roads will it get closer to what I am seeking? But it chooses to slide down by the left, and it seems to be drinking blood from the heart of Eva, blood slightly oozing, vitally throbbing like an emotion. Then, in order to acquire possession of two parallel states, it returns to the point of separation and takes off on the right, where love is calling. Here it needs the help of hands, and the contact of those thighs makes me feel as if I am falling suddenly into an abyss. Around there a remote thread of water runs toward her knees and feet. The reality of this brilliant ordeal wakes us up suddenly, and then we feel the urge to look at each other face to face, to confront each other in the entreaty that our two bodies are making at the brink of the abyss. Around us, at our back perhaps, there is a raging ocean. The noise is deafening, and its inundation seems inevitable. I feel the heat of something sharp in me, and I barely hear the voice that is calling me in anguish and in happiness within my bones.

For nothing resembles love more than this panic that explodes in the earthly body. "Your body knows it Eva, and nothing is extraneous or superior to you." And the fact is that she does not want to believe that her body has fallen into a world that is not mine. She cannot believe it. And without any effort, without any terror other than that of bliss, I lie down at the side of her living self, and I feel that with every movement of her breast she is sucking me in.

It could be said that at the window night is

waiting, and that the windows open in and not out to let the world see us interlaced and believe in our love and in nothing other than our love. And love pours out into the street and fills the city. Women enter their houses and lie on their beds, some without men. But soon after their job routines, or soon after those daily meetings, men arrive promptly to keep an appointment, for even if the appointment is a daily occurrence they cannot remember the exact details. Going home is like the beginning of a drama always to be renewed. It is because for us love moans in every bed in the world. Through the windows everybody has seen us abandon Paradise.

IN GENERAL—and excuse me for commenting on the authenticity of the joys and terrors that Eva seems to endure or into which she plunges—it can be assumed that she has to a certain degree dramatized her actions and her account of them, and that she indulges in some excesses of the imagination. I could also note in the margin of these pages a marked absence of facts, of necessary actions and telltale evidences of a possibly disorganized action, etc. I am tempted to submit these pages to a rigorously tight classification: I could also excuse myself and justify myself all along the way and in extremis relate in a very special manner a few days of the life of a woman and of a man without, precisely, entering into what is called the concrete details or lively manifestations of a psychic state. But why does one write a book? Whether I apologize or not, I must recognize the fact that in this case the curiosity of the reader is not going to be fully satisfied, but on the other hand it seems to me that I can bring about this time the secret and never truly confessed intervention of the reader into a narrative. On the other hand, in the daily flight sortilege and seduction reach, now as in the past, the dimensions of a desperate obsession.[19] It is not too bold to affirm, henceforth, that human beings run, now as always, toward an obsessive mystery as if toward a refuge. I invoke on this point, on the one hand, the concrete testimony of the psychiatrists, and on the other, that of the seductive awareness of the *voyantes*, etc. For this somewhat poetic climate of the self remains skin deep in relation to all circumstances. How does one decree its death? The fact is that Eva, or the most questionable kind of psychiatry, or the *videntes* are the cause, for the time being at least, for a feeling that I am not sure of being able to accept or reject.

Moreover, supposing that Eva represents the ultimate among beings that struggle desperately against these bedazzlements, I am inclined to believe in the authenticity of the images that fill her life and in their power to enlarge her domain. Yet how is one to explain the fact that she possesses a constant interior illumination regarding reality? I tend to think that her existence is somewhat akin to the world from which poetry might be said to derive. But actually why do I feel the need to justify? I am constantly asking myself that question when Eva calls at my door and I see her enter, her passage so similar to that of snow.

As they say in books, the afternoon is azure-blue, and the sun languishingly enters my room.

Eva's gloves are on a chair like deflated hands. I admire them in the dead solitude, in a dream of statues, and I observe that something of life that has slipped out of them glosses over the place like the passage of an insect. Eva herself does not appear too lively this time, and she is lying next to me, breathing with difficulty. Suddenly she sits up and her attention is drawn to the spot where there is a photo: "Homero Arce aboard the ship America." "A friend, eh?" Eva exclaims. But I feel sure that the photo was not precisely what awakened her, but something like a wanderlust or, better still, a sudden and desperate longing to travel. Moments later, my suspicion is confirmed in these sentences that unwittingly slip into her conversation.

—Do I have to tell you that my existence is consumed with a violent desire for flight? To flee!" And then, "I must admit that without you such a thing would be useless." And then, apologizing, "It seems to me that today I have lost the true direction of my feelings.

Yes, Eva. Everything in you is loss, I think. Your thought functions, this time, in the very same way as the sea. Your small waves stir, and, in order not to break, they fall flat on the beach. It is another way of saying: how can you account for the fact that your life is nothing but a flight?

As if to answer my reflections and questions, Eva continues:

—Would you believe that I don't like to startle myself?

Only once before, some time ago, have I as today tried to explain the asphyxiation caused by my feelings. I was traveling at night by train toward Talcahuano. During the night I had a great sense of happiness. Never had I been so happy. And yet, I did not know why. The following day this happiness was even more intense. The landscape was running inside me at a frenzied pace. I had an impulse to start conversations with the travelers. But suddenly the train came to the edge of a precipice, and everything changed for me briskly. It was as if I had suddenly awakened from a dream. I felt stifled in a heavy atmosphere where, oblivious to everything, the travelers were calmly continuing their lives. I closed my eyes. When I opened them again I looked at the travelers again one by one and, strangely, they were all focusing on *my* abyss. In that moment, someone cried for help from the bottom of his heart. And the truth is that, as I have said before, we are all nothing but a desire, and finally this desire—I could swear it—was plunging us en masse into a precipice. In those moments, I lost something of myself. I am sure that I alone responded to this collective cry! In the afternoon, the travelers left one by one or in groups at station after station. Each one, distinctly following my example, threw himself into *his* own precipice.

Disarmed and happy to hold her close to me, I saw her lying at my side again. Her desire was a small lamp in the darkness of my breast.

For two days I have had no news whatsoever of Eva. I have to confess that there is a vacuum inside of me. I am trying to overcome the importance I have been giving to my concern with Eva. An absence.

I know these absences in their minutest details, in their least visible traits. Her feet touch only difficult ground. I know the anguish with which she returns to my side and the terror with which she takes note of my unflinching loyalty, as she says. What will you think of me now? And, as always, she returns to seek refuge in my arms. Is it possible that it will always be like this? I see her closer to me than I am to myself. And then, as if being freed from a story or a dream:

—Do you see, Eva? If things were not like this . . .

Then I laugh out loud, and I have a feeling that her hands are cutting invisible flowers in the air, and then she trembles radiant as if a sun, which I do not see, were shining fully upon her face.

This kind of self-illumination is an act that Eva repeats very much in detail. And besides, for one thing, it produces in me an intense pleasure to see her enter into such a zone of radiant flowers; on the other hand, I must suppress in me at all costs an unknown current, one that is not at all far from a sense of asphyxiation. I remember her bleeding, as in that dream of the port under snow. I see her hands cut like two blue gloves, her undulating hair floating in the air, and the mouth paler than frost. In every way, it is to say, in the darkest confines of myself, a lamp is put out. There is no other way to feel the living contact of Eva, of that Eva a little anguished and totally unprotected. Then the reflection of her existence vibrates in the air. I see her growing, undulating, mingling herself with me and then dissolving in my veins in a flurry. Could it be said that Eva then enters, without great effort, into a state not totally unlike that of the *mediums*? One after the other I have heard her tell certain stories in unchallengeable detail, and they always begin,

—One day, in . . . , etc.

Then her pale little head falls on my shoulder as if into a well.

This happens quite frequently, and contrary to what one might think, Eva understands to what point it is possible to live in the margin of certain necessities, certain habits that it is almost impossible to forget entirely. How can one be useful to her under these circumstances? I ask myself. And I cannot answer except by trying to sustain and even to justify the almost perfect sense of liberty she musters at every challenge. And, to calm my spirit, I remember the happiness with which she appeared before me, for example, after an encounter with someone who must have been her *friend*, or with someone else, and as I see her reimmerse herself into the vision that burns within her it is difficult to reject the idea that she rises out of water.

Why create problems that in any case would not exist except with or without her(?) when Eva's freedom maintains no connection with any other, and when a natural appearance or the procedures that she finds are in most cases perfectly workable. At least as far as her passage through the world is concerned. For what purpose? I understand perfectly how difficult her passage is (life is not always a dream) and with what anguish she is forever chasing material existence and extinguishing certain fires to reach a state of sheer oblivion.

And if obviously there grows in me something strange, not alien to the emotion of love, these constant emergences from water produce in me a certain loss of what we pompously call "a sense of responsibility."

Naturally, however, Eva does not always give me the impression of remaining permanently upon flames; but quite to the contrary I would not think of following her to the far reaches of her existence where she comes close to the breaking point, for were she not oblivious of that stage her stay in this world would be largely jeopardized, in regard not only to her own being but also to the atmosphere that seems to have grown around her and me. Is Eva unaware that such situations produce a law of existence very much like a vicious circle? Believe it or not, this ardent flight through a world of oblivion is, possibly, the only shelter where one need not knock on a door or be obliged to identify oneself. Her feet surely must be entering into a zone of maximum despair; but where will she go, alone as she is among things? With a terrifying satisfaction I consider then what protection there can possibly be for her soul, that soul people would call "lost."

By the way, it is during one of these remissions of Eva to a point that may be called recuperation that, walking side by side one day, we note, both of us at once, that the ancient Plaza Otoman[20] has become a shelter unlike any other; that is why people assembled there clearly show a certain weariness, a certain diffidence, as if forced to live against their will and as if longing for a clear-cut collapse. As a matter of fact, Eva observes that there is nothing but *melancholy*, an inescapable, rampant melancholy that does not spare even the two or three traveling photographers stationed at the center of the plaza. A need or a feeling that we could or would not determine makes us pose for one of them. The sun shines directly on our faces, and I see Eva, smiling as she leans heavily on my arm. Five minutes later we look like an amiable couple on a postcard. On the back Eva writes "Eva and R. in the ex-Plaza Otomana" and a date. We leave the Plaza going north, and we cross a river. The water is running muddy as usual, and the sun falls directly on its bifurcations. Staring from the corner where the deserted Santiagian Luna Park begins, Eva encompasses with a penetrating look the perspective of Avenida de la Paz, at the end of which the building of the morgue is fully visible, and the dome of the cemetery. I suspect that Eva's mind is working in silence. Again the old caldron? Her eyes pale and sparkle at the same time, as if the weather were expected to change from one moment to the next. And in an odd way, I observe, moreover, that the sound of the water goes from Eva's heart toward the West.

As a matter of fact, in another luminous point of the day Eva returns to herself, if one may put it that way, and, perhaps remembering the wheel at Christmas, urges me to go admire the posters displayed on the houses alongside of Luna Park, where you could read "Bur Salón, Hotel El Marino," Bar "Colo-Colo,"[21] etc. You don't have to think of anything in particular to understand the clarity or the obscurity of these places, which are no doubt unpleasant to frequent but where with outstretched hands the poor seek refuge. Trembling with pity before the sad hang-out of the derelicts, Eva in a gesture of violence gives full vent to her rebellion against life and things, a rebellion toward which, as I have observed since, she harbors an almost desperate loyalty. Then, and as a logical consequence of her state of mind, I see Eva smile before the singular enchantment the signs of Hotel "El Marino" create for her. At the center of each one can admire one of those curious plastic achievements of popular paintings, an artistic genre unjustly neglected. But, if such is the impression, there is some other meaning that I cannot grasp, and Eva does not explain everything. But I understand perfectly the series of small dramas that are important to her—for example, the word "hotel."

We continue to walk eastward. I could be sure that Eva was again warming up her caldron. A few steps further, a story. "I think that my life really began when I was fifteen years old," she said. "I don't remember how, but on my way from home to school" (remember the "story" at the time she was eight, the snow, etc.) "I knew a man, not very young, but very determined. Actually, how is one to believe this? We were not different from others. His resolve and, clearly, mine carried us a little too far. That's when my 'crises' began, my encounters with the unknown and, what is better or worse, with my very self. For there is a house. From then on I felt very small, not a victim of anything, except of abandonment . . . for supposedly our resolute love swept us off our feet, as they say, beyond what is right or wrong. One afternoon . . .

it does not matter. Can you believe that, at times, I cannot forget that afterwards I came to know the first *hotel* and that its name was the Central?"

Yes, Eva, open your heart once more. I know the darkness in which it lives, the irregular pulse that drives it and that can be welcome only in special circumstances and for certain things. Your heart, so full of stories, so full and so empty, can reach out with that serenity it believes to be true or convenient now to my existence and to nothingness as well. You have been among men, you are always among men, and you expect no answer to the questions you ask yourself. Why? You walk on flames as if on land.

AT THE REPEATED requests of my friends Ignacio and Estéfano, I agreed at last, one day, to search the city for Bar Czaya II, which seemed to have unexpectedly disappeared.[22] But, in a few minutes, my attention was drawn to a number of towers that emerged at each step before our eyes. From that moment on I had something of an urge to detect a weak throb in my thought. With the appearance of each tower this thought bifurcated, escaped, flashed, galloped among the silent horses that, undoubtedly, draw the night along. With the last tower, Iglesia de los Sacramentinos, and without finding the Czaya, I began to think of the great capitals of the world, until my thought alighted upon one of them, *Moscow*. And I remembered suddenly the brilliance of Eva's eyes and the precision of her hand as she erased the date, the year 1917, that had been inscribed at the foot of the painting of Wladimir Ilitch, and to write in a color strangely characteristic of blood: *Year of Lenin*. She was in this simple and almost religious mood when we evoked that day the city of innumerable towers.

And in coincidence with the image of Eva and the towers, Estéfano Lombes said to me:

—Something is missing today among us three. What should not be missing? Is it something whose presence seems to confuse the better part of our reality?

—Yes, Estéfano. I feel a strange jolt, a sound that grows and fades away like this wave that reaches at times our ears, a wave that makes Eva exclaim time and again:

—Do you hear? —Death has just passed by. . . .

Although I must say that Estéfano referred in the intensity of his thought to something very vague or something quite similar, for example, to a woman, I cannot help but think that he added the following: "And Eva?" And here is another perplexing point. For it seems to me that my friend did not ask, "What happened to Eva?" but something very clearly suggesting "who is Eva?" But remember that she herself queried one day: "Who am I?" And quickly asking herself, "Who were you, Eva?" And the almost always nocturnal flower of her existence collapsed once on my chest. It is, no doubt, apropos of this secret and persistent question that the other day, in Eva's refusal to keep an urgent date—a date that, as I learned later, was almost of a horrendous necessity for her—she justified her refusal in no uncertain terms: "Why? *You*, Eva, are almost like something that does not exist."

BY ABSOLUTE CHANCE, by coincidence with a thought
that continually flashes through my mind, two
days later upon entering the Bar Jockey Club, I noticed that a certain more or less compulsive force
obliged me to retrace my steps. It is like an urge to
visit a friend, a plaza, a street, a bridge, finally a
thing or a point whose presence seems to inhabit
me unmistakably and tenaciously and of which I
am decidedly aware but which nonetheless I cannot clearly define. I walk back, and it is not easy
for me to cling to what could be called the irresist-
ible. Hundreds of men and women are taking
walks, until I begin to think that they are falling
out of all the corners of the afternoon. For behold,
here is the heart of Santiago, a heart somewhat in
ruins, for the time being, in its anxiety to become
a faraway reflection of the lights of New York or
Berlin. Right or left, the same surge of humans
floating in a dream clear or vague, but all-
consuming. Then the night begins to spread its
wings. From all directions the bright ads pin brilliant needles in the atmosphere. Twenty feet farther on I come upon Eva, seemingly in haste, alone
in the crowd.

—Is it possible? she exclaims. I have been looking for you for an hour. Some idea, you know what
I mean, gets into my head and makes me suppose
that you are not at home, makes me rush into the
streets. The city . . . Can you believe me, this time
I found a tune.

And again she lays upon my hands her gloved
ones. I notice in her a resurgence of joy and something like a revelation of positive happiness. And
again I admire that little smile that in Eva is like

a faint flame, and I am overawed by the way in which she overwhelms my somnambulant moments.

We are in La Plaza de Armas, and I do not feel like being dragged to the end of Merced Street.

—I have a surprise for you. . . . Do you know? You must know it. . . . A few blocks later Eva stops.

—My house, she says.

I see the stairs. They seem to be full of strange music, strange footsteps, and I seem to recognize the white stairway of our dreams. "Let's go up." Then I enter, once more, one of the residences of Eva's life, one of which I would never have thought "why?" or even in any way imagined. In the forefront a wide window that looks out upon the wall of Cerco Santa Lucía. And the rest, Eva.

Unhurriedly, and in step with the rhythm of nightfall, Eva repeats once more, and like a *medium*, all that related to her absences. Again the "clear-obscure" zone that seems to grow within her. Again the rich unconscious that sums her up and the convulsive course her mythical existence takes between my hands. It is as if years had passed, epochs, between her head and my arms. Then I begin to admire the small secret world—as secret as what?—of Eva. Suddenly I am trembling with surprise before a photo at the bottom of which one can read EVA in almost gothic characters.

—That's me when I was eight years old, she explains to me.

Immediately I remember the story of the boy dead in the snow. But my thought stops short. I re-

member that in 1911 I knew an eight-year-old
child who had an extraordinary resemblance to
this childhood Eva, somewhat rosy and, clearly, a
little sad. But the *voyance* of Eva prevented me
from pursuing this memory. For her my thoughts
held no secrets. Suddenly a strange melancholy
came over her; I heard her say:

—I think I see an eight-year-old child, rosy—
why rosy? Her name begins, I am not sure if it is
with an *N* or with *V*. I think it is *V*. You are a stu-
dent (she is not). In the afternoon you go home together. She cries, cries over anything. Her mother
is very dear to you. Her father is a foreigner. You
play a lot with V. But she cries, cries incessantly.
Nevertheless, now—I am not sure of this—she is
wildly happy.

The truth is that nothing I hear is false. And
this new intrusion of Eva into my thoughts and
into my memory casts a shadow over me, although
certainly not too great a shadow. Intentionally,
and as if wanting to change the subject, Eva returns to what could be called reality, or what is in
fact reality, mustering a smile that lasts for long
seconds.

—We could talk at length about this, she tells
me. There is nothing extraordinary about it. It is a
knack I inherited either from my mother or my father, I am not sure from which. Or from both.

Then, and because she lets slip two or three
sentences, I learn that her mother killed herself a
few years ago. I don't know whether she told me
this casually, but I did notice that she attached no
importance whatsoever to what might be called
preoccupations with the secret or secrets of her ex-

istence. She understands it exactly. In any case, my mind cannot avoid obstinately probing what has become like the clear conscience of Eva. Although the reflection of this search for destiny is reawakened daily, although the first movement of her heart is not daily directed by this concern, it occupies just the same a place that, without being preferred, absorbs all her lucidity, all common reality. Although I am certain of what I cannot confirm exactly, that in the time in which we are moving from one circle into another, through a small cross section of existence, she has always been totally lucid, I can recognize, even because of her certain horror of prejudices or vague symbols—justice, love, happiness, for example— that she has almost no desire either to leave what she herself calls "the come and go zone of despair." And all this does not happen exclusively at will, a thing that is almost on the verge of happening, but that at last happens. Eva does not care whether she is going in or coming out of it, except that she lives the better part of the time in a convulsive tension that is, I think, as if someone, pointing at an invisible spot, were to say suddenly: "The infinite."

Once the radiance of the photo of the child Eva is lost, I am the one who seeks refuge in an existence that is and is not that of Eva.

THE NON-STORY OF Eva, or the absolute impossibility of believing myself capable of becoming involved in affairs that belong to the world of fiction, compels me to follow a trajectory not unlike that which follows the ticking of an event about to ex-

plode. And the truth is that the premonition of
Eva's impending end is not identified by me, as
one might perhaps expect, with her death, but
with a violent entry into a difficult world, a slow
and sad departure of that Eva who can remain
close to me and see and hear day after day and, it
seems to me, day after day do it with increasing
love. After writing this, I thought how upon reading it she would reject the word "love" as if it were
a drug, although not always useless, but whose po-
tency she did not want to gauge. How can one de-
stroy in Eva this invariable rejection of what she
really is? In this night when the city sleeps so
tightly around me—I don't know why it should not
be otherwise—I disapprove of Eva's desperate indifference to the wavering feelings to which her
presence in my life subjects me. Thus, for instance,
she rejects the word "love" as she might reject
some myth, or some other sortilege whose radiance she considered to be involved in her own destiny. It would not be hard to refer to her difficult
passage through this world as *Eva or love*, and yet,
this would give me no access to any secret place,
nor would it be close to the truth when her
wounded soul has no support in hope: quite to the
contrary, how can one not believe that the world
has closed its gates on her? At this point one can
expect respectable people to moralize. But in
Eva's case nothing is gained by associating her
with slough.

Eva's loneliness keeps step with the slightly
sleepy rhythm of the night. The tall towers watch
over the sleep of those shining bodies that have
not known misfortune. But there is no doubt that

a good portion of the world seeks security under roofs, or in buildings, in streets, towers, police, and governments, etc. As if in compensation for its secret crimes, nature supports that loyalty and rolls out a splendid night in which angels wander here and there, rifle on shoulder or on wings. But can I say that I too exist, and that this good part of the world that reposes under the benevolent terrestrial and celestial loyalty has nothing to do with me? Have I the right to count myself among the good people who enjoy this great serenity? For let me not forget that around me there is another part of the world, hardly able to rest its bones. Its breathing is weary, and dream almost always, like the angels, bypasses these people, because they are disturbed by a load of horrors and visions. *This* is our world, Eva, and no other. We could affirm this with our hands and in our hearts. Its deep potential is about to awaken any day, even though your voice is no longer heard at my side, and even though mine will no longer be of any help to you. It is precisely when we are on the verge of a break between this world and the other that our thoughts embrace one another and our existence despairs of any imminent justice, of any imminent clarity. Why not think that there will be a day when your hands, instead of carrying roses, might carry guns?

Whether or not these words enter the realm of love does not matter.

AGAIN TWO DAYS without Eva. With distinct pleasure I observe that there is on my table a book of Augusto d'Halmar.[23] It is still half open, like a dream whose details take time to put together or have forever lost their way in the live jungle. I remember the avidity with which Eva read over these pages, in which a strange Lot figure encircled by visions was making its way with despairing sluggishness within her own disorientation. And what's more, I remember her looking with admiration at a small photo of the author of *A l'ombre des jeunes filles en fleurs*.[24] "Is it yours?" I said to her. And she put it away in a corner of her wallet, a place in which, it seems to me, if Eva were different, she would be carrying some secret drug.

I KNOW, I KNOW. I am incarcerated within four walls, and the prisoner that is inside of me can merely evoke the life that palpitates just the other side of the heavy bars of his cell. That is why this prison must be turned into a world peopled with beings and things that can coexist naturally in one's memory. There he was, and the terrestrial tune reached his ears. In the afternoon, for example, a woman! Is there anyone who does not have a woman? The two walk through the city, hand in hand, soul with soul. At least that is the exterior appearance. But surely there must be something more in this world of men, women, animals, and things. Still in the grips of the old connection, his thoughts crash against the iron bars. Then, there is only one man who matters, because he is sitting there at the very brink of oblivion. His feet, of his feet it cannot be said that they touch the ground, and his hands lie at the sides of his body as if in sleep. And love prevails. . . . Then the prisoner and

the self that is supposed to be me regain a single
personality at the contact of love. . . . As if around
me there was nothing but the remembrance of a
body. . . . I am surely thinking of my voyages
around her and of our constant shipwrecks. But
that is not all. And what of the absence of what her
vibration causes in things and in my actions? My
weak willpower leaves me defenseless. Somewhere
there are hands at ground level, like plants. There
are broken arms, floating. And eyes. There are ears
full of the sound of cries. And heads of hair de-
tached from their owners. What kind of a world is
this? What is one to do? Barriers, only iron barriers between us and something celestial like a sky.

Indeed, at the level of this brief knowledge of
the world of darkness, Estéfano Lombes approaches me. We begin to talk. The words come
out of a night almost completely similar to mine.
Then, between my friend and the prisoner who is
struggling behind bars, a dialogue begins whose
exact content I do not need to transcribe. But it is
not meant to be forgotten like a fantasy, for it
never ceases to be his inner host yet desires to enter once more the world; since he has come from
far, he seems to perceive between the two worlds
a point that is difficult of access.

And suddenly there is the voice that inhabits
Estéfano:

—For if it were not possible for us to speak of
death, I would not understand it, unless, for example, it was a thing or a being entering suddenly
into extreme radiance. I saw one day a dying person. At a given hour, his bed became illuminated
with a terrible green color. The sheets looked like

grass. The body of the sick person sought a position, was it its original position?—and, now calm,
as soon as he had taken a position, a supine posture, he began to enter what is called the agony,
which, in my opinion, is no other than the pleas-
ant and careful preparations we make at times for
a change, for an outing, for a voyage. The movements of the body were nothing more than the
movements of the hands that had control over everything, of the eyes that scrutinized everything so
that nothing would be forgotten, of the feet that
swept aside all useless objects. There may be a
number of forms of anguish, for example, that of
not being able to take along something more. This
"something more" could be a person, an object, a
tree one can see through the window. It can be a
slight pain caused by separation from certain
things. A form of grief, but not of despair. It may
even be nothing more than the physical discomfort
caused by the preparations for a voyage. And my
friend, what purpose would it have served us, supposing, for instance, that I had spoken to a dying
man as, according to Racine, Agamemnon revived
Arcas:[25] "Yes, it is Agamemnon, your king who
awakens you.—Come, recognize the voice that
strikes your ears." When my voice were to enter
his being, his body would have been deaf within
its excessive radiance. But when death . . .

And my voice from its prison:

—I see a world in the distance, in a dream
white in color. In the center of that world there is
something that belongs to me. The knowledge that
there is something of mine that is for the moment
not within my reach, I know that I owe it to a

dream or to a death. The truth is that there is in me a dream or a death. But it is through this experience that I have awakened in a land nourished, indeed, neither by dreams nor deaths, but by oblivion. How can I make you understand, my friend, that when my life is separated from Eva's, a night heavy with prison bars closes in behind.

Etc.

Afterward, Estéfano Lombes and I, somewhat reconciled—perhaps because we hardly understand each other—dance around the bed where I lie asleep and where the first hours of the night fall without the slightest noise. This dance is interrupted by the presence of Ignacio Brandez, who suddenly arrives dressed in green. He brings a few gifts, such as fruit, olive branches, red fish, and a bottle of wine whose bubbles we are unable to suppress. Then the dance is resumed. The three of us are moving as if in air, with hands clasped high and singing. But again we are interrupted by the arrival of another visitor.

—Hola, Samuel, come in!

And in truth, the latest arrival is Samuel. He is in black and stiff attire. His beard has grown thick. And for good reason, for Samuel has been dead for at least ten years. . . . Around midnight, I awaken. I have been sleeping for several hours with my head down on my work table. In the first instants I can hardly remember what I have been dreaming. I am aware only of the fact that I have several introductory pages where I am trying to express the despair that would be mine if I lost Eva. But later the dream—that is to say, what I have just dreamed—possesses me with such urgency that I rush into the street. The night is deep and high. A prison? Nothing happens in the world, nor in the night.

What can possibly happen in a prison and in the night?

Only in art is it still possible for a man driven by desires to do something that brings satisfaction.
—Freud

WOULD EVA RECOGNIZE herself in these pages? This is not difficult to predict. However, my hand is working away at an idea that can eventually be turned into the small radiance of this wayward Eva. Like the secret of a thought buried in the throes of darkness. Supposing that the sometimes equivocal existence of Eva had some relation to something that is happening in me—like the urge to write a book, for instance: one would have to admit that chance has made us victims of one of its singular games. But the apparent vagueness that resides in each act and even in each impulsive reflex of Eva does not stop having some point of contact with the arcana in which my being enters moments before working on the facts and the language of that life that is not totally subterranean, that flows from the passage of Eva at my side, as does the desire to fill these pages. Indeed, to dispel considerations so alien as to need proof of their validity, I come to the conclusion that there is an inconsistency in all my judgments relating to Eva's destiny. What seductive law does her apparition obey among elements that I was about to use, for example, to find a more or less temporary satisfaction?

I have hardly jotted down these reflections when Eva enters my room. Dressed in blue—and I calmly observe how her gloves and hat are about to be put down on a table laden with books. I understand that, except for certain items, the poverty of my home is not pleasing to her eyes. Just the same, I see her smile as if showing a certain temporary sense of well-being, for it occurs to me that her absences have taken after all a regular pattern, a development whose consequences at least do not seem to matter to her anymore. Am I right? It is not without apprehension that I think of solutions to Eva's problems, and those relating to psychic life are not the least difficult to figure out. As if my thought had stumbled suddenly upon the void like hers, I hear her say:

—It is incredible, but I think that I have found a way. . . .

It is possible, Eva. I know which are the only two ways at your disposal. It is easy. One in this direction, the other in that. I think of the weariness of your body and your ardent swimmer's hands. The sphere of your existence senses the end of its aimless twirling, and something other than illusion has entered your breast. By whichever road you go I have lost you. And how can I hold you forever in the void? Your thought and mine bypass each other blindly, though our hands are interlaced.

As if to leave this panic zone, Eva begins to browse through my books and to stop at certain pages, reading something out loud. I know perfectly well that she does not like everything in what we call the world of books. Guided by instinct, she flits from one place to another, from one book to another, like a wayward bee, although much too lucid. I see her drawing small circles in certain pages of the posthumous writings of Jack London, and the *Diary of a Writer* by Dostoevsky, in *The Artist as a Young Man* of James Joyce, and *Les plaisirs et les jours* of Marcel Proust, in *The Nights* of Young and *Remembrances of Childhood and Youth* of Renan, etc. No, no that's not it, Eva. But what world is there for you in all this, and what winds blow from your side? Suddenly I see her at the shore of a lake, looking a little pale in her blue attire, laid out almost touching the water, dead. The night falls promptly over the trees, over the church bells. Everything moves with a slow impetus. Everything is moving. Only Eva, is resting, by the water's edge.

When these images disappear, Eva is at my side, and her hands are resting upon mine. "I am not under any illusion," she says. "It would be hard to be fooled, but in the end I must choose a way out. I know what is called the impossible. Nevertheless, regardless of limitation—and in any case I am not moving out of the void—can I say that at your side, or away from you, I can hear myself living? Well, look at the lines of my hands . . ." Her hands were open wide. "After all, it does not matter." I hear her speaking as if in dreams and in a state that has ever been hers, and I understand that this visit holds for me something very much like a farewell. Her existence has halted. What kind of a halt is it? Actually, everything remains the same . . . minus your existence. *And what do you still have to live and to do?* (She points out.)

—And what is more, she continues, people say: I am going to die. How simple! And, nevertheless, it is not like that at all. You know perfectly well in what direction I can go, what course I am taking. Is the mental space clearing up? Is it in light or in darkness? In any case, its star is beginning to falter. And it is toward its star that my hands reach out, and they have now somewhat lost their way.

For a whole hour Eva continued this kind of talk, as much about me as about herself. Every moment there is a disconnected sentence, a shred of a thought, an image. And questions: "Lucidity ... what is lucidity?" etc. In truth, Eva is beginning to enter a phase where she is out of touch with me. I cannot stop thinking that there is a wall within whose enclosure are trapped certain wandering souls, a wall of diverse reflections that attract and repel, but a wall that at the end opens its fan made of stones. Not far from this space the woods of the mind grow, terribly wild, as does the penetrating atmosphere of dreams. In spite of everything, I reject once more the idea of seeing Eva swept away by this wind, caressed by those leaves, or in the proximity of the noisy, heavy hinges of these closed doors.

YES, I DO NOT succeed in my effort to reject the idea that the last and unexpected visit of Eva is for me very much of a farewell. I am returning again into a certain zone of intense disquietude, as if something or someone were holding me a little responsible for much that could happen to her from now

on. I think that a brief analysis of what I have succeeded in learning of her existence, and without
acknowledging that what happened between us
falls within the domain of love, would not lead to
the supposition that it was in my power to change
Eva's total and invariable destiny. It could be that
the night of her constant despair coincided with a
temporary pause in what could be called the triv-
ial events of my life. And even that the real urge to
act impulsively was of our own doing, having perhaps put us in contact in some way or another
with no closer a bond than that of common terrestrial despair. But is this love? I believe firmly that
my hand was guided by the presentiment that I
had to lose her. What more could have happened
after all that? I have seen her come from the
netherland or from the penumbra in which float
things and beings of invisible or subterranean life.
I have seen her approach my lamp without the
mediation of any sentiment other than the search
for firm ground, disputable and uncertain though
it might be. On the other hand I felt that Eva was
in me all that mattered, and I discounted any necessity to see her as anything else, that is to say, to
see her as a woman, for example, as a person of
mere flesh and blood. It is in this way that her
shadow holds in these pages a strict similarity to
the Eva that appeared suddenly in my life and the
Eva who seemed on the verge of entering a space
that, in spite of everything, I must not, nor do I
wish to, determine.

At this point, and always from a distance—
why?—from all the seeming signs of love, the
rather anguished tension of my thoughts does not

constitute evidence of the *uncertain* passage of
Eva's heart through the world. I think of a fall, for
instance in a place somewhat like this, like a
prison. I see her imprisoned, at last, in the name of
a terrible and always unjust social order, that false
and somewhat Machiavellian organization that
human depravity has encouraged and continues to
encourage so successfully, and that gives no little
satisfaction to the police and to the alienists. At
the same time, I cannot admit her sudden fall into
a world as nocturnal as hers, but where pleasure
would be for her as alien as, for example, love has
been. How can these two forms of collapse, seemingly so alike, be averted?

I happily discount, then, all signs of insanity in
the vague actions of Eva, all inclination toward
the easy life, and at the cost of what remains of her
physical radiance. But how can one stop her? This
obsession over Eva's fate begins to disturb me
somewhat. I no longer know what she does with
her days. I don't know how to free myself from the
feeling that what I experience sometimes is something of an exaggeration of her mental state. I just
can't imagine anything more difficult than not to
see her leaning over a precipice in no way illusion-
ary and to have the positive proofs of the impending disturbance that her suspicious disappearance
would cause.

THE BLOOD SPILLED on this page belongs to nothing
short of delirium, the vast delirium that grows
within me. I see it rising in a cloud of dust from
blinding winds. I hear its star glittering, ill-fated
yet admirable in every way. I hear the writing on

the wall. The fact is that it has been pursuing me since that date I have recorded elsewhere but which holds no particular interest today. But I can follow footsteps light as a breath, like a fire always on the verge of getting out of control. I know how long its despair took to reach the depth of my being. Its hand, which has not always been like a flower, has not ceased to keep out of my activities the indifference of all involuntary speculation. Can I state, then, that delirium embodies something resembling a great awakening?

I like to believe that very close to me there is a ripple that could well be from a small well with a star at its edge. Again, and I believe for the last time, the color red. For this well lets us guess her presence through a red circle. It is the color of fire, of anguish, of bullets, of the only climate possible. The color into which Eva has fled as if rushing, perhaps, to the stake.

Moreover, at this same hour and in a place that I do not seem to be able to identify, a flower is opening up its black corolla. I can hardly hear the sound it is making. A weak fire sparks my suspicion that a flower without a name is growing not far from the "cry for help" area of my vital zones. I can say, at least for the time being, that this suspicion is the heart of a flame that sounds like a heart in flight, time in flight, ocean in flight, night in flight, a hunting ground in flight, music in flight, a chorus in flight, a forest in flight, an angel in flight, dawn in flight, anguish in flight, death in flight, flight in flight. Immediately I turn around to see a tower leaning a little westward, a tower just seven years old which I last saw in this position quite a while ago. It is possible that this memory is trying to awaken some pleasure or some sadness of my childhood. In any case, its image, which comes to me as if from the depth of a precipice, runs in flight toward a radiance that can only be the presence of the excessively large hands that were extended to me at times by the strangest of my visitors. This visitor distinctly retained the appearance of a youth who whiled away his life in a hotel room in Valparaíso. I remember that this stranger regularly went to bed at dawn. His steps chased away the last ghost of the house. Then, I felt that—my room was next to his—he was watching and admiring everything and whatever was around him. That is why I can say that his eyes gazed more than on anything else upon a big, gorgeous wardrobe whose existence I began to guess until it became impossible for me to suppose that I was merely imagining it. (Why does a wardrobe almost always suggest a crime?) Shortly thereafter I would hear my neighbor begin to undress very slowly. Nevertheless, his clothes appeared to be always making a somewhat deafening sound. He would fall asleep in just about five minutes. Then the room would fill with echoes and strange radiances. It was as if in each part of the night he had to accomplish a hard task, a hard or sweet task, that of manipulator of dreams or of an assassin in flight.

But all this made me cover long distances, roads lined with black trees or cities with high towers. It is as if, at the hour when bridges guard the secret of the waters, my existence flees toward an unsuspected atmosphere. Or else that, at the very moment when my reason desires to tune in on a profound canticle, something like the overflowing of a liquefied flower, I would receive a letter from A,[26] my strange visitor, who, tired of what is known as "the world," finally retired to a convent in Calcutta. In any case, oh long night of heavy briquettes, in your wake I am nothing but a frail desire in transit or the depopulated dream of a dead man.

. . . How can we not recognize this current of air that is coming from somewhere and that is not some kind of hand beating in the void? From contact with this fire obscure plants grow, and the fury of its asphyxiating power floats from stem to stem, from petal to petal, with the light of a glowworm. Sometimes it feels as if the cooling of memory brushes away dead leaves in my breast, or as if my thought were suspended over a well full of water spiders. And it is as if a certain slow vapor were spreading over the terrestrial darkness. Its horrible tongues advance with deliberation to do their job, which discloses little by little a world almost at ground level, a world as faint as a breath. How can you not recognize that these low walls of the dream contain the dregs of Eva's footsteps? The admirable fire of her back spreads out, and her entwined arms extend around the brillance of her thighs. For the moment life on earth is determined by the dimensions of her body. The tallest plants are hardly able to flank her. She is stretched out, and over her breast walks the angel of love. But not more than two steps from her body the atmosphere begins to darken, and my brow lights up like an eye. And, what's more, there is a space where my being swings upon the waves. And the wind that comes from Eva—for it is none other than one of her winds—still brings a certain fire whose tongue makes the ashen night tremble as it falls asleep and into dream around her. Two steps from her world—and it is enough for me to know once more that it was not in vain that I was able to attract her love, which at this very hour can still overcome the secret asphyxiation caused by what has been and is the weight of the abyss. What new secret tears her out of her own oblivion? By the brilliance of her arms and the position of her feet, I am given to understand that she is entering something like water and that she is floating, for instance, over branches. And so she is out there somewhat dormant, no doubt, and radiant, over pale sands; and taking absolute responsibility for her destiny, she does not always comply with humdrum terrestrial laws. It is difficult for me to conceal the fact that I would have loved to see her there, from I know not where, and to have called her repeatedly by some name or other like the somnambulists. Or else, though I would not like to have been myself, but someone else, because how is one to make out the transcriptions of one's dream at the bottom of the water?

But things are not always so. I must admit that darkness sweeps away images, beings, and things, and although this may not be due to forgetfulness or fear, the small space in which I believe that I exist in one way or another is in fact despair with its game of illusion and which, as in the case of the floating body, appears to penetrate into a forest peopled with everything except life.

And above all, Eva, is it not true that nothing ever happens except in dreams?

... WHAT KIND OF a seduction does this impulse hold which began so slowly to invade what could be called the minor events of my life? Why is it impossible for me to capture permanently certain rays of a sun that I cannot identify, certain voices from the abyss, or the radiance of a day fully lived? Who is calling among those things that belong to me only temporarily? The most unknown part of my consciousness is present at that encounter, which is hardly more than the who passes? of the sentinel in the middle of the night. It seems to me that it is an admission that I am paying for an almost criminal act of which I am undoubtedly a victim. In any case, blind under my lamplight, I apologize to the daylight whose secret I think I violated under the protection of its own magic. I apologize to the magic carpet that more than once has raised me among presences not altogether alive but more than radiant. And which the alcohol of each night does not chase away, nor that of each dream in which I have harbored some desire, some anguish, something hated, something loved, something beautiful or something horrible, something living or something dead. This happens from the moment that I put my head down on the pillow of forgetfulness and that my total existence does not interrupt the brilliance or the music of high despair which is mine and which I cannot identify.

Now, depriving me decidedly of all intervention, there is still in my life an exit door, a sort of current of air largely charged by what could be my own reflection. This and the surprise attack, and the disguised thrust of an echo that I believe I can repel at the expense of the invisible, and even in some cases because I have succeeded in believing in the possibility of a permanent and difficult subdream. In this security and in this belief (coldly), I take inventory of the circumstances of my life. But around me the world quickens with life, and it is not easy to reject it as if it were fiction. Is it possible to believe in a life that rejects itself? I think I recognize this possibility unconsciously. And, precisely, with reflections from the zone in which the senses multiply there is something that Eva brought one day into my life.

Surely her warmth lingers on.

SANTIAGO DE CHILE, 1930

NOTES*

1. *País blanco y negro* [white and black country] (Edition ANDE, 1929), 86.
2. Valparaíso is a seashore resort on the Pacific coast of Chile not far from Santiago. It has many casinos and hotels and attracts not only fashionable tourists and vacationers but also artists. It is a picturesque site, with its rocky structure holding multiple levels of houses as if on a series of balconies with masses of flowers designed to border each cornice. (Ed. note.)
3. Salignac de la Mothe Fenelon, *The Adventures of Telemachus, Son of Ulysses* (Paris: 1811), 18:72.
4. Jules Supervielle, *Le forçat innocent* (Paris: Gallimard, 1930).
5. Today [1930] it no longer exists. It gave way to the Flower Market and the Arab Park.
6. Meaning: the short working hour. (Ed. note.)
7. *País blanco y negro* [white and black country] (Ande edition, 1929), 29–39.
8. Still life. (Ed. note.)
9. Literally "the forest of the florists," it was located where the Avenida Bernardo O'Higgins, Santiago's major thoroughfare, now lies. (Ed. note.)
10. Please excuse this particular reference to two of my best friends, a reference that throws absolutely no light on what they really are or on what they should be as characters, even circumstantial ones, of a narrative. With them it is impossible to reach an end to this feeling, were it because of the evanescence with which they appear and disappear in my existence—neither more nor less than Eva herself—as it turns out because, and always begging you to excuse me in the name of what a narrative could be, not one of them constitutes here any other need than

*The notes are Rosamel del Valle's unless specified as "editor's note."

103

the definite obligation and fleeting presence between Eva's environment and mine, and even in certain instances. How else can they be linked with this "vision" if not like two good images of somewhat unfortunate passage? Moreover, that nothing compels me to practice art in "red"—that is to see, live, with a red-hot iron.

11. A Chilean alcoholic drink. (Ed. note.)

12. In those days, and more than of Eva, of course, my thought was reduced to a constant evocation of a canvas: *The Assassin and the Dove*, by a German painter.

13. The Chilean poet was a constant companion of Rosamel del Valle in their early days, when they were attracted to the surrealist ambience. (Ed. note.)

14. Humberto Díaz Casanueva was another close companion with an attraction to surrealism. A poet of recognized stature in Chile, with a German Ph.D. in science, Diaz Casanueva was the ambassador to the United Nations during the Allende regime, and before that served in other diplomatic posts, as did Neruda, including a final post in Egypt. But given the choice after Allende's downfall between returning to Chile and giving up his traveling visa or staying abroad, he chose to return to Chile. (Ed. note.)

15. Neruda was at that time the ambassador to India. (Ed. note.)

16. That child with her hair to the winds who is running after her wooden hoop that, without being the "daily tragic," nonetheless does not fail to suggest the darkest melancholy. That is to say, consistency and purity. (One could add that this is the same painting which had so impressed the young surrealists Breton and Éluard, as well as being a favorite of their mentor Guillaume Apollinaire.) (Ed. note.)

17. According to a Latin American custom, when the new moon rises people take out money for good luck and hold it up toward the moon. (Ed. note.)

18. San Juan de Dios Hospital is a general hospital, near the Torre de los Diez. Neither one has any tragic association or literary connection. (Ed. note.)

19. Everything with the brilliance that modern "civilization" demands in respect to being and its existence. But nothing is accomplished without the obscure and untres-

passed zone of all the more than little surprises that the spirit guards day by day.

20. Today it is the Plaza Venezuela. (The author's "today" is 1929. Ed. note.)
21. Named after a football team of the day. (Ed. note.)
22. *País blanco y negro*, 86.
23. *La lámpara en el molino* (1914).
24. Marcel Proust.
25. Jean Racine, *Iphigénie*, act 1, scene 1.
26. Alvaro Hinojosa accompanied Pablo Neruda to India in 1927. Reference is made to this fact in a letter from Neruda to Rosamel del Valle dated July 28, 1928: "We are all the time with Alvaro, only a week ago did we separate and he went to Calcutta, having tired of Rangoon. There he lives in a Hindu monastery, surrounded by Vedas and Upanishad." (Ed. note.)

Designer: Linda M. Robertson
Compositor: Auto-Graphics, Inc.
Text: 10/12 Aster
Display: Futura
Printer: Maple-Vail
Binder: Maple-Vail